The Comic Book Kid

The Comic Book Kid

Adam Osterweil

pictures by
Craig Smith

Front Street
Asheville, North Carolina

For the children of Springs

Text copyright © 2001 by Adam Osterweil
Illustrations copyright © 2001 by Craig Smith
All rights reserved
Printed in China
Designed by Helen Robinson

Third printing

Library of Congress Cataloging-in-Publication Data
Osterweil, Adam
The comic book kid / Adam Osterweil ;
pictures by Craig Smith. — 1st ed.
p. cm.
Summary: When they are given an unusual comic book that
allows them to travel in time, twelve-year-old Brian hopes that he
and his friend will be able to replace his father's valuable
Superman comic that Brian had ruined years before.
ISBN 1-886910-62-6 (alk. paper)
[1. Time travel — Fiction. 2. Cartoons and comics — Fiction.
3. Fathers and sons — Fiction.]
I. Smith, Craig, ill. II. Title.

PZ7.O846 Co 2000
[Fic] — dc21   00-034835

Contents

I Tell You About Paul, Me, and My Deep, Dark Secret

It all started on a Friday a couple of weeks ago. It was a beautiful fall day, and I was trapped in English class next to my best friend, Paul. He's twelve, like me. On that particular day, Mr. O was teaching a lesson about how to develop characters for stories.

"Today I'm going to show you how to make your characters speak, blah blah blah," Mr. O lectured, scribbling a list of words on the blackboard.

There's a rumor that Mr. O used to be a rebel fighter in South America. He drives a beat-up car with bullet holes in the side. The other day he handed out sour candy and asked us to describe the flavor. Little did we know that the candy was imported from overseas, where people don't have very many taste buds—my lips turned inside out. We still have to get Mr. O back big time.

"Sleepover tonight?" Paul whispered to me.

Paul slacks more than anyone else in junior high. He wears size 40 jeans even though he weighs only ninety pounds. Mr. O says that slacking is useful because it cleans the floor.

"Yeah," I replied. "Bring your new comics."

"Brian," Mr. O snapped, "which of the verbs on the board best illustrates what you just said to Paul?"

"Replied," I replied.

"Excellent!"

Paul did come over that night, and we hung out in my room until the wee hours. Paul brought a pile of comics with him. Between the two of us, we have about five thousand comics. They're not funny animal comics, either. They're all cool superhero comics, like *Superman, Batman, Iron Man,* and *Aquaman.* I keep each one in its own specialized plastic bag because even the slightest wrinkle can lower the value of a

comic by a lot. I started collecting about five years ago, after IT happened. IT is my deep, dark secret.

"Bri, check this out, the newest *Superman* has a chromium cover," Paul said, flashing the shiny comic back and forth.

"Let's check it out in the price guide," I suggested.

Paul yanked the guide from me and quickly flipped through the pages.

"Phat," he said. "I bought it for two bucks, and it's already worth two-fifty. Cool investment."

He flipped through the guide some more until he got to the section about the golden-age comics, the old ones from the thirties and forties. They cost only ten cents originally, but now they're worth loads of money. Almost everyone from back then threw their comics out or stuffed them in damp attics. Most people didn't think to protect them—that's why they're so rare and valuable. Collectors will pay hundreds of thousands of dollars for certain golden-age comics in perfect condition. I used to get sick just thinking about that, mostly because of IT.

"Check out these old comics," Paul said.

I grabbed the price guide from Paul and shoved it under my bed. I had to—otherwise I was going to throw up.

"What gives?" Paul asked.

"Who cares about those? Let's steal a snack from the kitchen."

"Why do you always spaz when I look at the old comics? Give me back the guide." Paul reached behind me to get it. I tackled him, and we wrestled. When Paul finally got the book away from me, he drew a yellow smiley face on its cover and the words "What up, homie?" That was his way of trying to find out about my deep, dark secret. Well, it didn't work. I just shrugged.

After that, we forgot about the old comics and did sleepover stuff until the middle of the night. Paul and I competed to see who could invent the better superhero. I won with the diabolical Deathman. He's red with a black D on his chest in the shape of a coffin. A mad scientist named Mr. O built him, and he can create black holes with the wave of a hand.

It was all good until we went to bed.

You see, I had the nightmare again soon after I fell asleep. I woke up sweating. I must have screamed because Paul sat up in his sleeping bag, his braces glinting in the moonlight.

"Was that you?" he grunted.

"Fine, do you want to hear about IT?" I asked.

"What?"

"The story of why I hate the old comics."

"Uh, sure." Paul flopped on his back and made an angry noise. I could tell he really wanted to go back to sleep, but I finally had to tell somebody about my horrible past.

"I did a terrible thing when I was seven," I said. "You have to promise not to tell anyone."

Paul nodded.

"One day Mom and Dad left me with a baby-sitter who didn't really care what I did. I wandered into my dad's closet, where a black trunk caught my eye. I creaked it open, uncovering a gleaming treasure of old toys and games. I had never heard of any of them, including one called Howdy Doody—a bathroom toy, I guess. A shiny case peeked out from underneath the colorful pile. With one pull I yanked it free, revealing the coolest thing inside: *Superman #1* in *mint* condition!"

"No way!" Paul said in disbelief.

"I'm not kidding. It was my grandmother's. She

bought it when it first came out in 1939, and then she passed it on to my dad."

"I don't believe it."

"Let me finish. I was just a kid, so I didn't know that the comic was worth more than our house. The cover was shiny, colored in bright yellow, red, and blue. Superman flew up into the air above the streets of Metropolis next to the words '64 pages of action,' 'All in full color,' and '10 cents.' I was really excited. I got a big glass of fruit punch from downstairs, placed it next to the plastic case, and settled in to read."

"Don't tell me," Paul moaned.

"I slid the comic out of the case and opened it. Then the baby-sitter called up to me."

"I'm gonna be sick."

"I panicked, and the comic became a big glop of paper and punch. I rolled it into a ball and tossed it in the garbage, hoping to hide everything from the baby-sitter."

"Brian, go back to bed," Paul said. "You had a bad dream. I've known you *forever* and you never told me that."

"It's a deep, dark secret, like how Mr. O got his bullet holes."

"It *had* to be a bad dream," Paul said. "You have them all the time."

I ran down to the den, where Dad kept the remains of the comic under a glass dome. The only legible part on the ball of pink mush was the cover price of ten cents.

"My dad *hates* me," I said, plopping the ball into Paul's lap.

Paul stared at the comic ball with wide eyes, turning it around slowly. He flipped the price guide to the golden-age section. Sure enough, there was a picture of *Superman #1*.

"Listen to this," Paul said. "*Superman #1*, published by D.C. Comics in 1939, is valued at one hundred thirty thousand dollars in mint condition! Only three copies of this quality are known to exist ..."

I yanked the guide away from Paul, but this time he didn't fight back.

"That comic cost only ten cents in 1939," Paul said. "Do you realize what a messed-up investment that was?"

I didn't sleep much that night. Paul was now the only person to know that story besides Mom, Dad, and the baby-sitter. He kept telling me how lucky I was not to be in jail, until he finally fell asleep. I stared at the shadows on the ceiling for half the night, trying to imagine what it would be like if I hadn't discovered that little box in the closet.

We Get Something Strange at the General Store

Mr. O says that setting is important to a story, but you shouldn't describe every last detail because it gets boring. If you describe a town, you shouldn't describe every rock in it. If you describe a house, you shouldn't describe every spoon in it.

It's the year 2001. I live in a small town called Springs, which is on the eastern end of Long Island. It has one school, a church, a meeting hall, and the General Store—they all sit around Parson's Pond. The rest of the town is mostly houses and forest surrounded by bay beaches on three sides. The fourth side borders East Hampton, where a lot of rich and famous people live. There's no mall anywhere near here because developers haven't heard of this place. We don't even have a traffic light. My house is old, and I have a bunk bed in my room. Done.

The next day Paul and I had plans to walk to the General Store to check out the rack of comics, but first we had to eat breakfast with Mom and Dad.

"Full brightness!" Dad shrieked at me, shielding his eyes. He always makes jokes about how my orange hair gets oranger as the sun comes up. He's got a bald spot, so I don't know why he goes there.

"It'll blind us!" Paul added, turning his head away.

"Too late! Fling this into my mouth to reverse the damage," Dad directed, placing a Cheerio in my spoon.

I accidentally launched the Cheerio into Mom's hair, where it disappeared into the tangles. Paul and my dad spent a long time giggling about it.

"That's a weird spoon," Paul said to me, trying not to laugh.

"Why don't you tell Paul where you got that spoon," Mom teased.

"Who cares about a spoon?" I said, embarrassed. "I got it at Disney World when I was five. It has Mickey Mouse on it wearing a diaper. Are you happy?"

"What are you guys up to today?" Dad asked.

Paul was staring at him, waiting for the raging, comic-loving, Brian-hating beast to emerge. It wasn't like that, you know. He didn't always show it, but I knew Dad hated me for destroying his most valuable possession, and no flying Cheerios were going to change that.

"Nothing," I said gloomily.

"I'm going to make a ten-dollar bill magically appear," Dad announced, reaching a hand toward my ear. He snapped his fingers, but his hand remained empty. He frantically searched around for the bill.

"Here it is," I said, fishing a green blob out of my orange juice. Dad has to be the worst magician ever.

"Yes, well, we're going to a party in East Hampton, so get yourselves a pizza for dinner," he said, squeezing the juice out of the bill.

"Lights out at ten," Mom said sternly. The Cheerio fell out of her hair and skipped under the table.

On the way to the General Store, Paul told me that I was nuts. "Yeah, your dad *really* hates you," he sneered. "Come on! Your dad kicks—he's always happy."

"He's always in a good mood when other people are around," I explained.

A bell rang when we opened the door, and we walked over to the rack of comics in the corner. The General Store has been around forever. Old Mr. Somerset, the owner, always tells us that he was born right here in the discount section. Mr. Somerset is awesome. We've worshipped him ever since he took us for a wild ride on the beach in his Hummer. He's like one of us kids, except old.

"Maybe someday I can retire off these," Paul said as he piled up the chromium-covered issues of *Superman*.

"You don't even have a job," I said impatiently, trying not to think about IT while I flipped through a copy of *Batman*. I wasn't in the mood to buy any comics, but it was always cool to check out Mr. Somerset.

"'Sup, Mr. S?" Paul asked.

"What do you think, boys?" Mr. Somerset said. He lifted his sleeve to reveal a tattoo of a Hummer next to the words "Yep, I own one."

"Wicked!" Paul gasped.

"What's the trouble?" Mr. Somerset asked me as he wiped the counter. "Nobody with orange hair should be sad." Whenever he spoke, fuzzy clumps in his ears moved back and forth. I seriously thought about warning Mr. Somerset not to get an earring, no matter how cool he is. No Hummer can make ear hair look good.

"Nothing," I mumbled. "I had a bad dream last night, that's all."

Mr. Somerset stopped wiping and stared at me with a look of disbelief.

"I've been waiting to give you something," he said vacantly, creaking his bones over to a chest. He pulled out a shiny bag containing a comic book, blew some dust off of it, and returned to the counter, staring blankly. His fixed gaze looked right past me as he carefully handed me the comic. I thought I saw a red flash, and then Mr. Somerset looked me straight in the eye and said, "Now grab a Coke and be gone with you."

On the way home, Paul and I stopped at a patch of grass to check out the comic. Gold bubble letters spelled out "TimeQuest" on a blank silver cover.

"Let's open it," Paul said. His hair flopped over his eyes while he ripped the plastic security bag off the comic. You can't see Paul's eyes when he's excited.

"Look at the cover price," I said. "'Two purple coins.'"

"That's gotta be a misprint. Maybe that's what we're supposed to find. Maybe Mr. Somerset is testing out a design on us."

When we turned the silvery cover, two small metal squares fell out and landed in the grass. *Blank* comic panels filled the inside pages. No story. No pictures. No ads.

We scrambled back to the General Store to ask Mr. Somerset about the comic, hoping maybe we could trade it in for another *Superman* or something. A sign on the door read "Closed for Beach." Mr. Somerset, strapped into his Hummer, was speeding off toward a wooded trail.

"The comic's blank, Mr. Hummerset!" I howled after him.

"I've often wondered," Mr. Somerset's voice floated back. Then he disappeared into the dunes.

"He's weird," I said to Paul.

"Yeah, sometimes I think he's a wizard," Paul confessed.

It was too nice out for comics, so we got our skateboards and jumped the curb behind the school for the rest of the afternoon. After a while, I even forgot to be unhappy.

We Discover the Dangerous Truth About the TimeQuest Comic

Paul convinced his mom to let him sleep over again that night. I'm allowed to stay home without supervision now because Dad said I already wrecked all the breakable stuff that isn't insured. Also, Mom insists that no bad people have set foot in Springs since Captain Kidd buried his treasure here in 1699. We never even lock the front door.

After my parents went out, Paul and I sat on my top bunk and stared at the TimeQuest comic with bewilderment.

"Look!" Paul said.

Different images appeared on the cover when Paul moved it around. It wasn't like those magic pictures that change once or twice—dozens of scenes showed kids fighting aliens, battling creatures, or just talking to people.

Suddenly the comic disappeared, only to be replaced by strange red words whizzing around. Hundreds of these words created the comic's rectangular shape, but they moved too quickly to read. After a red flash the comic reappeared, whole again. Paul and I stared at each other in astonishment.

We flipped through the comic and found some writing on the very last page:

TimeQuest Ring Instructions

Step 1: Make sure the ring is glowing *green*. After each use, the ring will glow *red* and take between one second and one week to recharge.

Step 2: In a clear voice, tell the TimeQuest ring what year you want to travel to. Be sure to specify "A.D." or "B.C."

Step 3: Press the TIMEQUEST button in the center of the ring for activation. You will now warp to the time indicated on the digital display. Anyone holding a TimeQuest coin will join you on your journey.

Step 4: Press the HOME button to return to your home time. To travel to another time, start back at step 1. See restrictions below.

LIMITATIONS: Cosmic pathways are limited. Once you travel to a specific date, you may not travel to within one hundred years of that date using the same TimeQuest ring. Example: If you travel from your home time of 2499 A.D. to 2404 A.D., you may not travel to any time within the range of 2304 A.D. to 2504 A.D. again, with only one exception. You may *always* travel back to your home time of 2499 A.D.

WARNING: At the core of the TimeQuest ring lies a complicated computer program nestled on a microchip. This technology is still developing. Volunteer children have experienced headache and dizziness while using TimeQuest merchandise. One small dog exploded when a child volunteer tried to take it back in time. Remember our safety motto: "Fluffy doesn't *need* to see the past— *he's* just a dog." As well, changing the past may unpredictably shift the course of time. TimeQuest Incorporated is not responsible or liable for the alteration or destruction of life as you know it.

I fumbled around in my pocket for the little metal squares that had fallen out of the comic earlier. One was an adjustable ring attached to a metal backing. The front of the ring had a big button labeled TIME-QUEST and a smaller button labeled HOME. A digital display scrolled the message "Thank you for purchasing TimeQuest merchandise." The ring glowed green.

The other square contained four punch-out coins labeled TIMEQUEST. Tiny letters on the coins read:

Home (always allowed): 2001 A.D.
Visit the Yo-Yo Emporium today!

"Are these for real?" I asked.

"They're just CrackerJack toys," Paul answered. "Let me show you." He yanked the ring out of my hand and said, "Seventy-five million B.C."

"Wait!" I tried to wrench the ring back from him, but he had already pressed the TIMEQUEST button.

"See, it doesn't do any—"

We tumbled through the air and hit water with a warm splash. I scrambled to the surface and took a breath. I couldn't see land anywhere, only crashing waves all the way to the moonlit horizon. Strange squawks echoed across the dark water, and shadows swooped through the sky.

That's when I remembered a terrible thing: Long Island wasn't around seventy-five million years ago. We were floating in the Atlantic Ocean!

My legs felt like logs from trying to kick heavy jeans through the water. Suddenly, slacking didn't seem so cool. Just when I was about to go under, something growled and swam between me and Paul. I imagined the headlines in the future: *Scientists Find DNA from Boy in Ancient Fossilized DeathRaptor. Teeth Marks Show He Never Had a Chance.*

"Press HOME!" I screamed, scrambling to stay afloat.

I felt teeth grip my left pant leg. The beast yanked

off my jeans and devoured them with a foamy gurgle. A moment later we found ourselves in the basement of my house, lying in a pile of dirty laundry. A bra sat on Paul's head like a bonnet.

"Mr. Somerset *is* a wizard," I said. "The ring works!" I looked down at my soaked boxers and wondered how I would explain my missing pants to Mom.

"No," Paul returned. "He's a superhero. Don't you see, the General Store is his hideout. He uses it as a base for fighting evil, and that beat-up Hummer is like his Batmobile."

"I guess," I said, motioning to Paul about the bra. "But there is no evil in Springs."

"That's why he's stuck helping out depressed kids," Paul continued. "That's what superheroes do when they retire, like start charities and stuff." He picked up the bra between two fingers and slowly moved it away from his body.

I looked down at the TimeQuest coins, which I was still clutching in my hands. They read:

Home (always allowed): 2001 A.D.
Forbidden: 74,999,900 B.C. to 75,000,100 B.C.
*Try our new always-flavor gum in the
CandyWarp Zone!*

"How is he helping by getting us attacked by a sea monster?" I asked.

"'Cause we're going to use this ring right," he declared, lifting a pair of pantyhose out of my hair.

"What do you mean?"

"We're going to use it to get another copy of *Superman #1*," Paul said in a very serious tone.

I stared at him for a second while I let this sink in. The idea of going back in time again worried me. Getting devoured by a gurgling, jean-crunching beast was not a very appealing thought. Then I imagined how happy Dad would be when he found out I replaced his comic.

We ran up to my room in a flurry of excitement. Paul climbed onto the top bunk and grabbed the copy of the TimeQuest comic. I put the ring and coins in a plastic bag for safekeeping.

"Wicked idea," I said to Paul. "You're a genius."

We Plan Our Journey

When I woke up the next morning, I looked around my room to see if it had all been a dream. The TimeQuest comic lay in the middle of the floor, and my slimy clothes sat in a pile in the corner. The whole adventure had been real! I opened the comic to take a closer look at the instructions, only to see that pictures and words now filled the first page.

One panel read, "Our tale opens as Mr. Somerset gives the TimeQuest comic to two unsuspecting boys in the remote town of Springs." A few panels showed me and Paul checking out the comic and going off to skateboard. Another panel showed us sitting on my top bunk reading the instructions. My wavy hair looked exactly the same in every scene—I use too much gel.

The next panels showed Paul pressing the button, followed by the word "ZAP." Then: "In the murky Atlantic Ocean, 75 million years ago, our heroes battle a slimy sea monster." My eyes opened wide when the sea monster ate my pants.

The last panel read, "In the nick of time, our

heroes warp home. What will happen next in the daring adventures of Brian and Paul, Boy Superheroes? Turn the page to find out."

I turned the page, but all that was there was one lonely box showing a picture of Dad hunched over the wrecked Superman comic, crying like a baby.

I dropped the comic and ran down to the den. I was relieved to see that the TimeQuest comic had been wrong about Dad crying. He was just sitting at his desk reading a newspaper.

"You don't have to go to school tomorrow if you get this in," he said, throwing a foam ball at my face. He likes to play basketball with a little plastic net on the wall.

I missed by a mile. I have terrible aim, so Dad knew it was a safe bet.

"Oh well, it's school for you," he said, staring at me with his big, alien eyes. When I was seven, I asked Dad what planet he was born on, and it made him laugh for a long time. I remember it well because it was after IT happened, so it was good to have Dad laugh with me again.

We played basketball for a little while, but then I ruined everything. "What if I told you I was going to replace *Superman #1?*"

"Not again," he moaned, dropping the ball.

He didn't say anything else for a while. I could hear my heart beating above the silence.

"Did I ever tell you about the time I lost Grandma's diamond earrings?" Dad finally asked.

"Yeah, you were trying them on, and they fell down the drain."

"Never mind how it happened," he snorted, blushing. "The point is, you need to forget already."

"I'm gonna get that comic, you'll see," I vowed.

I glanced over my shoulder as I left the den and saw Dad remove the wrecked comic ball from under the glass and stare at it with sad eyes. Then he hunched his face into his hands as if he was about to cry.

So the TimeQuest comic records the past *and* predicts the future! I ran upstairs to look at the magic pages, but no new drawings appeared. I desperately wanted to fill those blank panels with me replacing

Dad's comic.

I woke Paul up. We wrote a detailed list of everything we would need for our journey, along with a step-by-step plan for getting the comic. I wanted to go right away, but Paul said that he would get in big trouble if he missed his orthodontist appointment on Monday.

The next day in English class, Mr. O put me and Paul on opposite sides of the room so we couldn't talk to each other.

"Every story has a bunch of problems, large or small, that keep the plot going—they're called conflicts, blah blah blah," Mr. O lectured. He gave the class an assignment to invent a small conflict for a story. Well, our plans really excited me, so I wrote a note to Paul instead of doing the classwork, and then I folded it into a triangle.

Mr. O walked up and down the aisles to check up on our work. I waited until he turned his back to Paul, and I hurled the note. There's only one problem: my aim stinks. It spiraled around like a dying bird until it hit Mr. O and fell to his feet.

When he realized the note was for him, Paul yelped and dove at Mr. O's feet.

"Nice shoes," Paul said, looking up with a smile of braces. Then he put the note in his mouth.

"Perfect!" Mr. O said. "We have our first conflict. Can anybody tell me what the problem is?"

Kara raised her hand and said, "Paul's lying at

your feet because Brian hit you with a note. Brian's face is bright red."

"And how might I resolve the conflict?" Mr. O asked.

"Uh, send them both to the principal's office?" Kara answered.

"But we could avoid that if Paul hands over the note, I would think," Mr. O offered.

Paul spit out the note, wiped it off, and handed it to Mr. O.

The class giggled as Mr. O opened the note and read it aloud: "'We could get in major trouble if somebody notices we're gone, so we'll have to wait for the perfect time tonight to warp. Tell your parents that you have to sleep over to work on a project ...'"

"This is good work, Brian," Mr. O said, waving the piece of paper. "But please, in the future, refrain from folding up your classwork and throwing it at my back."

Mr. O walked to his desk, mumbling something about early retirement.

We Set Out to 1939

Paul and I planned to escape unnoticed after my parents went out for dinner that night. In the meantime, we packed everything we needed for the journey.

"I think we should wear overalls or some other dorky thing," I said, worried about how the sea monster devoured my jeans. "They didn't slack in 1939."

"Nah, maybe we'll teach them a thing or two," Paul replied. "Does your mom ever give you a problem about it?"

"No, she always says I look phat and messed up."

"That's cool. My mom told me I look like a homeless person."

"Grab that bag of dimes," I said, pointing to the dresser. "We'll need one to buy the comic."

Mom and Dad walked in as Paul dropped the heavy bag into his giant pocket.

"No mischief tonight," Dad said.

Paul's pants fell to the floor with a jingle.

"Don't worry, we're working on a project for English," I reassured Mom and Dad, hoping they wouldn't notice Paul's yellow boxers.

"It better not involve dumping any more seaweed in the laundry pile," Mom warned.

After they left, Paul agreed to ditch his jeans, so we put on some old overalls that I dug out of my dresser. I slid the ultimate protective case for *Superman #1* into my front pocket—guaranteed to be waterproof, airtight, shockproof, and non-biodegradable. Paul stuffed the comic guide into his pocket. Then I gave him one TimeQuest coin and slipped the other three into my overalls along with some of the dimes.

We took one last look at the TimeQuest comic. More panels had filled in since the one about Dad crying. One showed Paul diving for the note at Mr. O's feet. The caption read, "Our heroes narrowly escape trouble at the hands of the villainous Mr. O, known throughout the world for his diabolical Detention Ray!"

On the next page, a kid rocketing through space fired lasers at a fleet of alien spaceships. The ad read:

**Are you ready for an uglee
drax adventure?**
*Try playing SpaceMaster today in the Adventure Zone!
It's so deranged, you'll think you've clyved!
(Sponsored by SkankyKandy,
the makers of Programmable Gum)*

We climbed up to my top bunk.

"Ready to warp," Paul said, holding on to the sides of the bed.

"1939 A.D.," I told the ring. The year appeared on the digital display, and I pressed the TIMEQUEST button at exactly 5:55 P.M.

A moment later the bed quietly disappeared from under us and the ceiling changed into a sea of chipped paint. Paul looked at me like a cartoon character that knows it's about to fall off a cliff, and then we crash-landed on a girl in overalls.

"Hey!" the girl squealed.

Everybody panicked and scrambled to separate corners of the room. The girl hid behind the door and stared at us with large brown eyes.

"Are y-you … Martians?" she stuttered in a scared voice.

"We're from the future," Paul answered.

"Are you going to zap me … or—or something?" she asked.

"No. We … uh …" I noticed a pile of comics by the bed, so I said quickly, "No, we're comic collectors like you."

"If you're r-r-really not Martians, p-prove it," the girl stammered. "Um … tell me who appeared in the first issue of *Marvel Comics*." I spotted *Marvel Comics #1* just lying around like an old shoe.

Paul flipped through the price guide and said, "Sub Mariner, Human Torch, and Kazar the Great."

The girl walked out from behind the door. She was pretty short, and she still looked scared. "Kazar's pretty thrilling. I was just on the first page of

Superman when you crashed on top of me. You wrecked my comic."

I gasped when I noticed that the girl was holding a crumpled copy of *Superman #1*. Suddenly I felt sick. I pictured myself standing before a judge.

"For the protection of comics everywhere, I sentence you to life in prison," he said in a deep voice. Hundreds of comic collectors cheered as I was dragged off in chains.

"You guys owe me a dime for my comic," she said. "I'm Mattie. I'm twelve."

"I'm Paul."

"Brian."

We all stood around like dorks not knowing what to say. I'm pretty shy about meeting girls, so you can imagine how I felt, trying to socialize with a strange girl that I fell on sixty years in the past. Talk about mad awkward.

Our Plans Go Terribly Wrong

Mattie's room had uneven walls, lopsided windows, and absolutely no electronic equipment. She had only a single bed instead of a bunk bed, which explains why we fell on top of her.

The only cool thing in the room was Mattie's pile of comics. She had all the old stuff, the kind that collectors would die for in the future: *Detective Comics*, *Action Comics*, *Famous Funnies*, and *Donald Duck*. All of them had a cover price of ten cents, and they still had glossy covers. A million dollars' worth of comics just lay there in her little pile.

"Did you guys say you were from the future?" Mattie asked, scratching her bowl of black hair.

"We're from the year 2001," Paul explained. "We came to get a comic book."

I told her about my father, his wrecked comic book, Mr. Somerset, and the magic TimeQuest comic. I even showed her the ring, which sputtered a worrisome rainbow of colors.

Puzzled, Mattie looked up at the ceiling and said, "C'mon, guys, aren't you really from the circus? Can you teach me how to tumble through the air the way you did?"

We had to show Mattie something else from the future quickly.

"Show her your braces," I whispered, elbowing Paul. He smiled.

"That doesn't prove you're not from the circus," Mattie said.

Paul stopped smiling and showed off his sneakers that light up when you take a step.

"So, clowns wear big floppy shoes that glow in the dark."

"Nice overalls," Paul said angrily.

"Thanks, yours too," Mattie replied. "Who cares, anyway. What do you guys wanna do? I don't get many visitors."

"What do you do for fun around here?" I asked.

"Mostly I play games with Video," she said.

"Video games? But ..."

"Video!" she called, crossing her eyes. A little one-eyed dog shaped like a wrinkled squirrel entered the room and hopped onto Paul's sneaker. "Video, meet Paul and Brian, they just dropped in."

"Cool, a mutant," Paul said as Video chewed on his shoelaces.

"I named him after a new invention that lets you send an electrical picture through the air," Mattie explained. "I was going to name him Toto from that new picture show, but he doesn't look like a Toto."

He didn't look much like a Toto or a Video to me. Paul was trying to kick him off, but with his teeth clamped to Paul's laces he flopped around like a limp rag.

"Oh, here's a splendid game," Mattie sang, grabbing a paddle with a ball attached to it. She paddled it wildly, grinning from ear to ear like she was having all the fun in the world.

"We gotta get you outta here," I said, patting Mattie on the back.

Mattie's mom entered the room just then. She had big brown eyes like Mattie.

"Oh, hello," she said. "Who are you?"

"We're from the circus," Paul uttered nervously, hopping on one foot. Video went flying and landed on *Marvel Comics #1*.

"I knew it!" Mattie screeched.

"The circus is ten miles away," Mattie's mom said.

"I've never seen you two around here before. Are you with those outlaws hiding in the back woods?"

"No, honest, we're circus performers," I said.

"Well, come eat supper with us, you're all skin and bones. My husband's away helping our cousins rebuild from last year's hurricane, so there's plenty of food to go around."

For supper we ate clams, oysters, and bread in a room that smelled like sawdust. Metal baskets filled with vegetables hung from the ceiling.

"What did you do in school today?" Mattie's mom asked, spooning out peas.

"Nothing," Mattie said with a sigh.

"We don't go to school," Paul said. "We're circus freaks."

"What do you *really* do in the circus?" she asked, looking at us suspiciously.

"I pick up after the elephants," I said anxiously.

"I juggle," Paul answered.

Mattie's mom handed three apples to Paul and said, "Prove it."

I looked around for an escape, but that mutant squirrel blocked the only exit. He devoured a bowl of food in one gulp and blinked his eye.

"It's all good," Paul said, grinning. He threw all three apples into the air at the same time. One landed in the oysters. Another landed in the clams. The last one landed on Paul's head.

I imagined an antenna rising out of Video's head.

"*Crusty Mutation BX-Alpha to home base,*" he barked. "*The liars have arrived. Supper will begin in thirty seconds.*"

"I was beginning to worry that you were with those outlaws," Mattie's mom said. "But no son of an outlaw would be that bad of a liar. Don't be ashamed that you pick up after the elephants too, Paul."

After dinner, Mattie's mom told us stories around the fireplace. She was an expert on the past, and she had hundreds of scholarly books to prove it. Even her tales couldn't cheer me up, though. We had been away from our own time for only a few hours, but I missed home a lot. My parents and friends hadn't even been born, yet somehow life went on as if it wasn't even looking forward to them.

The worst part came at bedtime. Mattie's mom wanted us to quit the circus, so she told us that we could sleep on a pile of rags in the basement if we *promised* to go to school the next day—perhaps the worst deal in the history of humankind.

We Go After Superman #1

The next morning Mattie dragged us to school. The building didn't have a cafeteria, an auditorium, dismissal bells, or locks on the lockers—just like Springs School in the year 2001. When we got to class, a teacher named Mr. Miller called out names for attendance even though there were only six students. Then he sprayed everybody's homework with disinfectant and collected it. There's obviously some rule that you have to be weird to teach junior high in Springs.

"This is Paul and Brian," Mattie explained.

"If you can't read or write, I'll send you down to elementary," Mr. Miller cackled. "Never seen a kid with metal teeth. Are you with those outlaws I've been hearing about?"

"We're not outlaws. We're brothers," Paul said, smiling at me.

"You don't look like brothers."

"He's adopted," I said, glaring at Paul.

During social studies, when we were learning about the history of boredom, Paul passed me a note about our plans. Unfortunately I didn't get to read it

47

because Mr. Miller snatched it out of my hand and bellowed, "Class, eyes closed!" louder than I'd ever heard anyone yell.

Everybody closed their eyes except me, and then Mr. Miller hit me on the knuckles five times with a ruler. It hurt so much I thought I was going to cry. Paul cringed each time the ruler hit my hand.

"I don't know where you boys go to school, or if you do, but there are strict rules in my classroom," Mr. Miller said, spraying the ruler with disinfectant.

If that wasn't punishment enough, I had to clean erasers during recess while Mr. Miller slept in the classroom.

"Something bad happens every time we say we're not outlaws," Paul whispered. "Next time I'm gonna say that we *are* outlaws from the back woods."

"Outlaws don't wear dorky overalls," I said, banging erasers together. The chalk dust created a yellow streak across Paul's face. "Anyway, we have to stop lying."

During math, Paul squeezed his nose while trying to clean the chalk off his face. He had to sneeze big time. When Paul sneezes, it sounds like an African wildebeest giving birth on a nature program.

"What do you get when you multiply two-thirds by five-eighths?" Mr. Miller asked Paul.

Paul squinted but said nothing.

"What … do you get … when you multiply … these two fractions," he said slowly, walking over to Paul.

"Haven't you been paying attention at all?"

"GraaaaaahhhhhSPLOOOOTCH!" Paul answered.

I could almost hear the whispered voiceover of the narrator on the nature program. *"And there you heard the ritual cry of the African Paulibeest. Watch how birds scatter from nearby trees as the sound echoes through the canyon."*

Mr. Miller was covered with snot.

The next few minutes were pretty scary as Mr. Miller sprayed himself with disinfectant. Paul looked at me and Mattie for help, but it was hopeless. Mr. Miller waved the ruler like it was a lightsaber. He snarled, and I saw fire in his eyes as he approached Paul …

After school, I tried to cheer Paul up by reminding him about our step-by-step plan to get *Superman #1*. Step one: Put a copy of *Superman #1* in my indestructible protective case. Step two: Zap home. Easy. As we walked to the General Store, though, I became a little worried about step two because the ring still sputtered.

A bell rang when we entered the store. Mannequins wearing dresses stood by the counter. The smell of shoe polish mixed with fish made me gag.

"Hello, Mattie," a man said. "I set aside a special honey stick just for you. Bees with brown eyes made it."

"Thanks, Mr. Somerset. Meet my new friends, Paul and Brian."

I couldn't believe that this was the same Mr. Somerset who would drive a Hummer in the future. For one thing, he didn't have any ear hair. A mustache curled around his nose, and he looked serious, like all those people in old black-and-white photographs.

"Did you get your car yet, Mr. Somerset?" Mattie asked.

"Not yet, but I picked out the color," Mr. Somerset said, pulling up his sleeve to reveal a tattoo of an antique car. "Black—the color of the raven, the night sky, and my heart."

"Wow, can I get the first ride?" Mattie begged.

"You got it!"

We walked toward the back of the store. Coffee grinders lined the shelves, and big iron spoons hung from the ceiling. A sign on the wall read, "Try *Stephen's Cold Cream* for bedsores." My heart started beating fast when the rack of comics came into sight.

It looked like a regular old rack, but the shiny comics on it were worth millions—*Jumbo Comics, More Fun Comics, All-American Comics, Adventure Comics,* and of course *Superman.* Old comics have much more interesting covers than new ones. We have holograms and stuff, but even that's not as exciting as the words "THRILLING! SENSATIONAL! ACTION-PACKED!" on a colorful cover next to a price of ten cents.

Paul was afraid to touch any of the comics. Even

a fingerprint could reduce the value by tens of thousands of dollars. Dad's *Superman #1* was in mint condition. Not a scratch, bend, or tear.

"Hurry," Paul whispered. "We have to get back home."

I turned the rack so that the glossy cover of *Superman #1* was facing me, and I prepared to pick it up. It was the last copy in the store. One wrong move, and I wouldn't get a second chance.

"Gloves," I said, holding my hands up.

Paul grabbed some thin gloves off a shelf and put them on my hands. Mattie looked at us curiously.

"Protective case," I said.

Paul pulled the case out of my front pocket and

then held it up, opening the top flap. I carefully lifted *Superman #1* out of the rack and prepared to slide it into the protective case. Just then Paul's nose began to twitch—I had to think fast. Paul sneezing was definitely not part of the plan.

"Put a laundry sack over his head *now*," I ordered when I saw Paul's eyes go cross-eyed.

Mattie slammed a sack over his head just in time. An explosive "GraaaahhhBLOOOF" puffed the sack up like a car's air bag.

Mattie held the sack away from her face and said, "This sack should go in the discount section now."

Paul's face was bright red, but he held his hands steady enough for me to slide *Superman #1* into safety. I took a close look at the comic after Paul snapped the case shut. Perfect. Except that one piece of hair was stuck inside.

"Let's go!" I commanded. We ran back through the aisles.

I plunked one of my dimes and the comic on the front counter.

"Very mysterious. I never saw anybody treat a comic so well before," Mr. Somerset said.

Paul was about to respond, but I put my hand over his mouth. I was afraid he was going to say, "We're freak brothers. I'm Sneezy, and he's Brian."

Mr. Somerset took a close look at the dime. That's when our plan fell apart.

"Into counterfeiting, are you?" he accused. "This

dime doesn't look right at all, and it says 1999! Are you with those outlaws hiding out near the coves?"

I picked up the comic and backed away from the counter. Nowhere in our detailed plans did we discuss the possibility of being mistaken for counterfeiters.

"Yeah, we're outlaws," Paul said. "I'm Paul the Kid." He gave me a proud look, as if he had prevented us from getting in trouble.

Just then a shadowy figure walked through the door. He grabbed the bell so that it didn't ring, and then he clanked toward the counter in his big boots.

"What … what can I do for you, sir?" Mr. Somerset stammered.

The man grabbed the sack from Mattic. "Fill this with food and a fresh pair of overalls, and maybe then I don't get angry," he barked. His hat hung low over his face so that only his crooked lips and scraggly chin showed.

So outlaws *did* wear overalls.

"Can't an honest man earn a living in peace?" Mr. Somerset said as he ran quickly through the aisles, dumping supplies into the sack.

"Empty those pockets, kids," the man ordered.

I nervously splashed dimes onto the floor, and Paul threw the comic price guide at the man's feet. Hoping the outlaw wouldn't notice, I held on to

Superman #1 and the three extra TimeQuest coins.

"This is my lucky day," the man said, staring at all the dimes. He knelt down and gathered them.

"Hold this," I whispered, handing a TimeQuest coin to Mattie. I pressed the HOME button on the sputtering ring. Unfortunately, the ring beeped, and a message scrolled across the digital display: "Primary system failure—rerouting power to backup processor …"

Mr. Somerset returned with the sack full of supplies and handed it over to the outlaw.

"I'm taking these kids fer insurance," the man said gruffly. "If I hear one barking dog after me, they get hurt." He pointed to Paul and added, "This guy with the funny teeth is first."

I always thought it would be exciting to be captured by an outlaw, but at that moment I wished I was curled up in bed reading a comic book. My legs trembled as he led us toward the front door.

The Outlaw Traps Us in His Hideout

Before the outlaw led us out of the General Store, he grabbed a handful of honey sticks, gave one to each of us, and put the rest in the sack. I know, I know— I shouldn't have taken candy from a stranger. But I already knew that this stranger wanted to hurt me, so why not have a honey stick first?

"Those'll keep yer mouths shut for a while," the man grumbled. He pushed us onto a wooded path that darkened only a few steps into it. "Doggone sugar'll rot your teeth, but what am I, your mama?"

As we crunched through the forest, I stared at the cover of *Superman #1* every few seconds to make sure it was real. Paul tried to get my attention.

"Warp…already…press…the button," he muttered.

"Tried…ring's broken," I muttered back.

Eventually we came to a rickety old cabin in a clearing, probably a mile from the nearest house. It was gloomy inside, and armies of bugs marched across the rotting floor. The outlaw sat each of us down in a different corner of the room.

"My name's Joe," he said, tying our wrists and feet

together. "My friends call me Ugly Joe on account of my temper."

He plopped himself down next to Paul and took off his hat, revealing a mostly bald head covered with the words "WELCUM! FRUM JAKE."

"My son done that while I was sleeping," Joe said, pointing to the sloppy green writing. "Jakey thinks the Martians'll see my head first when they arrive, and he wants to make friends with 'em. That little scamp gets crazy ideas from his radio programs."

"My dad's going bald too," I said timidly, hoping to show him that we had something in common. "I once drew a bull's-eye on his head with markers."

"I ain't bald!" Ugly Joe insisted, feeling the clumps of hair above his neck.

He walked over to me, grabbed *Superman #1*, and then settled back down near his sack.

"Jakey read this to me," he said, trying to open the case. "It's about this strong feller who come here from another planet. I could get an honest job if I had muscles like him, but Jakey says it's swell having an outlaw fer a dad."

When Ugly Joe popped the case open, my heart started beating fast. If he put even one of his grubby fingers on the comic, my whole plan would be ruined. Paul looked at me in a panic.

"Ohhhhhhhhh, I'm not feeling well," I moaned, trying to distract Ugly Joe from the comic. "I'm so hungry!"

"I told ya that candy is bad fer ya," Ugly Joe said, dropping the open case. "Let's get ya some proper food to settle yer stomach." He fumbled around in the sack. Anybody who would go to such trouble for a kid had to be a nice guy.

"There's slime in this sack," he said, scraping out the remains of Paul's sneeze.

Mattie cringed as he licked his finger clean.

"Mmmmm, honey," he observed, retrieving the rest with a knife. He fashioned it into a snot sandwich.

"Uh … I'm not hungry anymore," I said, staring at the sandwich.

"Bah, kids can never make up their minds," Ugly Joe said, taking a bite. "Anyone else want some?"

Mattie and Paul shook their heads back and forth as the sandwich dripped.

"Then I'm gonner relax a bit," he said, reaching his slimy fingers for *Superman #1*.

"I'm hungry again," I said desperately. It was either the comic or *me*.

Ugly Joe scrambled over, held the sandwich to my face, and said, "Here."

Now *this* was definitely not part of our plans. *Step one: Get Superman #1. Step two: Get kidnapped by outlaw. Step three: Eat Paul's snot.*

"Yum." I gagged nervously. Paul looked at me with only the white part of his eyes.

After forcing myself to swallow, I heard barking in the distance. Ugly Joe ran outside to look around.

"I'm gonna puke," I said.

"We're caught!" Ugly Joe announced, storming back in. His feet knocked the comic back over to me, and I immediately picked it up and snapped the case shut.

Just then my sputtering TimeQuest ring beeped. "Backup processor activated, warping in five seconds …" scrolled across the digital display.

Moments later Video ran through the doorway and leaped into Mattie's lap. Then the cabin and forest disappeared around us …

?????????

????????

We sat on a patch of dirt in the bright sunlight. Bushes and grass covered the landscape, dotted here and there by round pines sprouting out of the ground like pimples. The bay sparkled under a wispy orange sunset, and a swampy smell filled the air.

"Gee whiz, what happened?" Mattie asked, cuddling Video.

"We went through another time warp," I explained as we freed ourselves from the ropes.

"*Another* time warp?" Mattie gasped. "You mean you guys really *are* Martians or from the future or whatever?"

"We told you," Paul said casually. "Brian, what year are we in?"

"I don't know. We're definitely not home."

When we stood up, I showed Mattie and Paul the scrolling message on the sputtering ring: "Backup processor failure—Destination: *Unknown*."

"But I have to get back," Mattie whined. "I'm supposed to go to the World's Fair with my dad this weekend. They have swell inventions there."

I felt terrible about taking Mattie out of her own time, so I didn't show her the tiny words on the TimeQuest coin:

Home (always allowed): 2001 A.D.
Forbidden: 74,999,900 B.C. to 75,000,100 B.C.
1839 A.D. to 2039 A.D.
????? B.C. to ????? B.C.
Try our new sense of warmth in the Emotion Zone!

We walked toward Parson's Pond. I carried *Superman #1*, still in mint condition inside the protective case. Before long, a strange squealing noise floated over a nearby hill, along with the pounding of feet. A furry cross between a gorilla and an elephant emerged, kicking up dust and speeding toward us like a runaway train. In a panic, I dropped the comic and dove behind a boulder for safety.

A boy holding a spear chased after the creature, yelling, "Soota!" and "Kooma!" The gorilla-elephant trampled past me, but the pursuing boy slipped on my comic and fell to the ground, allowing the animal to scamper off to freedom.

"Wow! A giant sloth," Mattie explained. "I read about them in one of my mom's books. They went extinct ten thousand years ago."

"You mean we're in prehistoric Springs?" Paul marveled.

"Hutty foo!" the boy hollered, kicking the ground

with his heels. He wore animal-skin shorts, and he was about Paul's size, with messy brown hair.

I grabbed *Superman #1* and hid it behind my back.

The boy stood up and pointed to himself, saying, "Mai-kee, Mai-kee."

"Hi, Mikey."

"Bana," he said, waving for us to follow him.

We hiked to Parson's Pond. At the water's edge, fires spewed twirling white smoke, and children chased each other around rickety huts. An old woman holding an ivory spear walked toward us as we approached. She wore a fancy hat made out of a sloth's head.

"Mai-kee," the old woman yelled, stopping at a

safe distance. "Soota?" She pointed toward a fire and
then at her mouth.

"Hutty foo," Mikey said, pointing to my comic
book.

"Kalu, bana!" the woman shrieked, raising her
spear in the air. Men and women wearing animal
skins emerged from the huts and gathered behind the
old woman.

Mikey walked over to me, grabbed the comic, and
ran over to hand it to the woman. The villagers huddled around the comic, murmuring. Soon Mikey led
me over to the crowd. I was scared even though
everyone stared at me in awe.

The old woman put her hand on my shoulder.

"Soota," she said, making an eating sign. "Dinta," she added, pretending to sleep. Then, pointing to the picture of Superman flying up into the sky, she said, "Weni." She hopped up with outstretched arms, which made everyone laugh except me. "Weni," she repeated, pointing to me. Finally, pretending to stab something with her spear, she shrieked, "Kooma!" Without another word, she disappeared into a rickety hut carrying my comic.

"What did she say?" Paul asked.

"We're gonna eat, and then we're gonna sleep," I said.

"Good," Mattie said. "I'm hungry, and so is Video."

"And in the morning I'm going to fly, or she's going to kill me."

Nobody made a sound, not even little Video.

I Get Caught in a Great Battle

After a sloppy dinner, when the moon sent a white streak across the pond, the madwoman put us into a guarded hut. I gave the ring to Paul since I didn't know what was going to happen to me in the morning. At least if it started working again, he and Mattie would be able to warp to safety.

"I'm going to click my heels together three times, and I'll appear back home with Mom and Dad," Mattie said. She banged her shoes together over and over again.

We didn't say anything for a while. The crickets reminded me of lying in my safe bed after getting tucked in by Dad. Finally Paul started a conversation.

"What's your favorite television show, Mattie?"

"They're going to have television at the World's Fair," Mattie said excitedly.

"Never mind," Paul said, rubbing Video on the head. "What's your favorite sport?"

"Baseball," Mattie answered. "I love striking all the boys out."

"Yeah, baseball's cool," Paul agreed.

"What's *your* favorite thrill?" Mattie asked.

"Sledding down a big hill," Paul answered. "Nothing beats the rush from cold air and snow."

"Gosh, you guys still do that when you live?" Mattie asked. "Sledding is keen. I have a black sled called 'Midnight Rider.' I've had some grand spills."

"What's your favorite smell?" I asked.

"My mom's pancake batter!" Mattie said.

"Cut grass," Paul said.

We had the wickedest conversation for half the night. Then Mattie and Paul fell asleep, and my terrible fears came out. Would we be stuck here forever? What were the villagers going to do to me in the morning? Were Mom and Dad already searching the forest for me with police dogs? I tossed and turned until morning amid a chorus of unfamiliar insects.

I thought about that awful night five years ago. After I destroyed *Superman #1*, I pretended to be asleep in my room, hoping nobody would notice what had happened. When my parents came home, Dad walked into his room and dragged the trunk out of his closet. There was silence for a minute—then an earsplitting cry and loud footsteps toward my door...

In the morning, Mikey ran into our hut, saying, "Tani, tani." He held a small rock to my face.

"Cool rock," I said groggily, trying to humor him. His toys were even worse than Mattie's.

"Tani," he said again, tapping on the rock. The rock split into two halves, and a small lizard jumped out onto my arm. Mikey thought it was very funny when I screamed.

When we stepped outside the hut, an armed tribe led by the madwoman took us on a scary march through marshes and fields. Looking sad, Mikey tagged along. The journey ended on a large rock jutting out over a steep cliff. When I looked down at the muddy bottom, I saw birds with webbed wings flying *below* me.

The old woman pointed to the picture of Superman flying, and then she threw the comic off the cliff. She was *serious*.

"Weni!" she yelled, thrusting the spear at me as if I was walking the plank. Villagers held on to Mattie and Paul at the old woman's command.

"Bana, weni kooma," Mikey whined. He squeezed

his way through the crowd and tried to pull me from the edge, but a sad-looking villager yanked him back.

"Please, I just want to go home," I begged, holding my jittering hands together. Paul pressed the HOME button over and over again, but nothing happened.

The madwoman had run out of patience. She shoved me hard with the side of her spear, pushing me off the cliff. At the last moment a strap on my overalls snagged itself on a sharp edge and swayed me like a pendulum over the swamp below. Wearing overalls was a pretty good idea after all, I thought.

"Weni!" the madwoman cried, hacking away at the strap with her spear.

The strap broke, of course. As I soared toward the swamp, my stomach felt like it was plummeting down a roller coaster. The last thing I saw was Paul and

Mattie looking down on me with miserable faces, and then a muddy sponge squeezed around my body.

I quickly pushed my head out of the bubbling soup. Four wolves lurked on a flat rock only ten feet away from me, each the size of a refrigerator. Rows of knifelike teeth lined their bulging jaws. I stood perfectly still for a few minutes, hoping the creatures would get bored and leave.

"They're dire wolves!" Mattie's voice suddenly came out of nowhere. "They'll eat you!"

"Good poochies. Poochies want a back scratch?" I

laughed nervously. The wolves began growling at me.

I turned to escape and saw a radioactive elephant from an evil scientist's experiment. Its ripped, flabby trunk sprouted hair and large pimples.

"And that's a mastodon!"

The wolf pack wanted the mastodon for dinner. I was caught in the middle, which made me the appetizer. I finally understood how terrified Kaanga felt in every issue of *Jungle Comics*.

The wolves plunged into the bubbling ooze, and the mastodon rumbled toward me with stumpy feet, its rough hairs trailing behind in muddy clumps. I tried to get away, but my overalls were filled with muck and debris, making it difficult to move.

A shadow fell over me. The mastodon had caught up to me in only a few steps! Its ancient eyes looked off to the side in an uncaring trance, and its tusks gleamed like sharpened knives.

The wolves erupted from the mud and climbed onto the mastodon's back, where they gnawed furiously. I stood frozen in awe at the most action Springs has ever seen. The mastodon desperately swung its tusks back and forth until it finally fell next to me with a thunderous splootch. In the explosion of mud, *Superman #1* flew into the air, bounced off a wolf, and then floated alongside the mastodon.

"Yes!" I shrieked, forgetting about the monsters.

Determined, I reached my fingertips toward the hard case. Surely those giant creatures wouldn't

notice me. The comic was almost near enough to grab when the wolves got mad—not mad cool, or mad fun, *mad!* A dire wolf climbed onto the mastodon's head and howled at me with all its might. Pieces of flesh hung from its teeth.

"I was just leaving," I said fearfully as a burst of adrenaline swam through my body. I quickly abandoned the comic and waded toward the flat rock with newfound energy.

"C'mon, hurry," Mattie urged, peeking over a nearby hill.

I pulled myself onto the rock and stumbled into a nook behind the hill, where I watched the rest of the fight below. The dire wolves feverishly swarmed until the mastodon stopped moving. One wolf lifted its head toward the sky and gave off a final howl, as if to say, "Got milk?"

"Most of the villagers cheered when they saw that you were alive," Mattie explained. "Then that scary woman with the spear yelled something, and they all ran toward Parson's."

"How are we going to fix this ring?" Paul asked. It still sputtered a rainbow of colors.

"Give it to me," Mattie said, snatching the ring. "I'll fix it the same way Dad fixes things." She started beating it against a rock.

"We can't leave without the comic," I insisted. "We'll wait here until the wolves leave."

Paul and Mattie just stared at me.

"I think that was the breakfast bell," Paul said. "Look."

A large family of dire wolves walked out of the woods. Mother wolves held tiny babies in their mouths. They ambled toward us in a steady rhythm, staring with glassy eyes. They stopped a few feet away and stood perfectly still.

"Ring's fixed," Mattie sang, handing it to me. It glowed green, and the words "Backup processor functioning" scrolled across the digital display.

"Hit the button," Paul said nervously, staring at the wolf pack.

I pressed HOME, holding the two remaining TimeQuest coins tightly. Just then the remaining strap on my overalls snapped, flinging the tiny brass buckle toward the wolves. My overalls fell to the ground with a muddy squish as one of the wolves leaped at us ...

Home Again

My finger was still on the TimeQuest ring when we appeared in a playground near my house. A girl dangled from the monkey bars and stared at my boxer shorts.

As we ran home, I noticed that the sun was sinking even though it was morning when we left prehistoric Springs. The clock in my kitchen said it was 5:58 P.M. on Monday, only a few minutes after we had left for 1939. Mom and Dad were still at dinner!

Mattie wandered around the house, fiddling with everything, while I dug through my dresser looking for some pants. Then Paul and I opened the TimeQuest comic and eagerly read about our adventures. A big green "THWACK!" appeared as Mr. Miller hit me with a ruler. One panel showed large drops of sweat dripping onto Video as I slid the comic into the protective case. The story really made us out to be very brave, with captions like "THRILL as our heroes face a lawless bandit" and "GASP as Brian battles prehistoric dire wolves with his bare hands!"

An ad showed a blond-haired kid typing on a small

keyboard attached to a pack of gum:

Tired of the crowds in the CandyWarp Zone?
Would you rather choose the flavor
you swive in the comfort of your Base Zone?
Now you can with
SkankyKandy Programmable Gum!
Choose from such swixy flavors as
Metallic Gem, Cooty Grape, or Digital Delight!

I turned the page quickly—so far, nothing good had come from eating candy.

A caption on the next page read: "Will Mattie and Video return to 1939 to see their worried family again? Will Brian recover *Superman #1* from prehistoric times and make his father happy again? Find out what the <u>future</u> holds in the fabulous second part of our story."

Mattie wandered up to us carrying a picture and a remote control.

"Look, it's me," she said, pointing to a faded black-and-white image of a young girl. This picture had hung in the downstairs hallway all my life, but I had never taken a good look at it. The girl looked just like Mattie.

"Do you have to type in a secret code to use this ray gun?" she asked, holding out the remote control.

"That's for the television," I said proudly, clicking the power button.

"Oh boy," she exclaimed.

I flipped through the channels, trying to find the most violent movie to impress Mattie. I couldn't decide between *Friday the 13th* and *Nightmare on Elm Street.*

"Turn it off!" Mattie cried, covering her eyes. She turned away and asked if I had a paddleball.

We had fun for a little while reading my comics. Mattie couldn't believe that *Superman #400* cost

more than a dollar. She read dozens of my Superman comics, trying to catch up on everything that had happened since the first issue.

"The future's cool, I guess," Mattie said after a while, "but I want to go home. My parents are probably worried about me."

Paul and I looked at each other helplessly.

"Do you think I can go home now?" she asked,

cuddling Video. "It was swell on Saturday nights. Dad made malteds and we read about history."

"I can't lie anymore," I said. "You're stuck with us until we figure something out. Watch." I told the ring, "1939 A.D.," and pressed the TIMEQUEST button. There was a loud beep, and a woman's voice sang: "Incorrect use of the TimeQuest ring. Syntax error at line twelve million three hundred thousand and four. See instructions for proper usage. Thank you for choosing TimeQuest Incorporated and have a nice day!" The ring glowed purple for a few seconds, and then it changed back to green.

At that moment I heard footsteps on the creaky stairs. In a flurry of whispers we hid Mattie and Video on the top bunk underneath the covers. When Mom and Dad came in, Paul and I tried to act casual.

"I thought I heard a woman talking," Mom said, glancing at my pants suspiciously.

"Flight 740 is now boarding for Paultown," Paul sang in a high-pitched voice.

"Why are you wearing corduroys?" Mom asked me, straightening my pants out.

"Well, a sea monster ate my jeans, and my overalls filled with mud and fell off in prehistoric Springs."

"They're comfy," I said.

"Well, you look neat," Mom said admiringly.

"Can Paul sleep over?" I asked, scratching my leg. "We have to work on a story for English."

"I don't see why not," Mom said.

"Don't stay up too late, it's a **SCHOOL NIGHT** tonight," Dad said. The light from the hall lamp lit up his bald spot like a moon.

"And make sure you warp the space-time continuum and zap home that girl you have stashed under the covers," Mom added.

Later, we planned our next move by the glow of a flashlight.

"Look," Mattie said, pointing to the TimeQuest comic.

The next panel appeared, showing us sitting

around and thinking. It read, "Our brave heroes sit around and think. They wonder what the, ahem, FUTURE! holds for them."

We pondered this for a while. Then Mattie snapped her fingers and opened her brown eyes wide.

"Guys," Mattie said in a rising voice, "I got it. We have to go to the future."

"That's it!" Paul said, slapping his hand with his fist.

"Why do we have to go to the future?" I asked.

"It says so right here," Mattie explained. "'What the *future* holds.'"

Just then another comic panel appeared. The caption read, "BUT WAIT. WHAT'S THIS! ..."

We waited up half the night, but no more panels filled in, not even one that read, "THRILL as our heroes wait up half the night with a flashlight!" We were very curious to know what those words meant. But after the owls stopped hooting, when the only sound was the sleeping sigh of Video, Paul and Mattie fell asleep.

I lay awake, remembering the night Dad came storming into my room holding the gooey comic and wailing louder than ever. I tried to think happy thoughts about Dad to make the memory go away. He sometimes gives me a Super-Tuck-In at bedtime by shaking my body back and forth until I'm dizzy. Sometimes it's followed by the Tickle Torture, which makes me beg for mercy. Then there was the time he colored my arm with markers to make a black-and-blue mark magically disappear. I fell asleep thinking about these things ...

We Make a Terrible Discovery

We had no idea what time to warp to in the future, so Mattie, Paul, and I ended up going to school the next morning. We took the comic in the hope that it would give us another clue during the day. Video sat in my backpack along with my books. Mom looked bewildered when Mattie walked out the door with Paul and me.

In English, Mr. O asked us to take out our homework assignments and sit in groups of three.

"Did you make a major conflict for a story?" Paul asked as we pushed our desks together.

"Yeah, I wrote it out while that madwoman was hacking away at me with her spear," I answered sarcastically.

"Oooh, unprepared," Mattie teased, shaking a finger. "You're going to get whacked with a ruler."

We soon forgot about the homework and flipped through the TimeQuest comic.

"What year should we warp to in the future?" I asked.

"I say 3001," Paul said. "That sounds cool."

"No, 4444," Mattie offered. "Four is my lucky number."

"Guys, we can't just make up a number!" I argued.

"Do you guys have a problem?" Mr. O scolded, walking over to us.

"Yes," Mattie said. "I'm stuck in the future because our time-travel ring has rules, and I have to get home to the past, except we can't figure out what year to warp to in the future."

"Good work!" Mr. O praised. "That's an interesting conflict for a science fiction story." He gave us a candy bar.

As soon as Video smelled the chocolate, a low growl rose out of my school bag.

"Rowf, *rowf,* frowr, *groff!*" Video yapped. My bag teetered back and forth on the floor. The whole class fell silent, and everybody looked at our group.

I panicked and dropped the chocolate into my bag, where a feeding noise erupted. Soon the bag turned quiet, and the class resumed work.

"So, what year are we going to warp to?" Paul asked, turning back to the comic.

"Look, '2499 A.D.' is underlined in the instructions, just like 'future' was," Mattie noticed.

If you travel from your home time of <u>2499 A.D.</u> to 2404 A.D., you may not travel to any time within the range of 2304 A.D. to 2504 A.D. again, with only one exception. You may *always* travel back to your home time of <u>2499 A.D.</u>

"That's gotta be it," I said. "This comic knows everything."

"Awesome." Paul's hair flopped over his eyes.

"Then let's go there," Mattie said desperately.

"We have to wait," I warned. "We can't just leave in the middle of school."

In social studies, the tyrannical Mr. King ordered us to take out our homework. I was afraid to reach into my backpack because Video ate everything in there, including the Wite-Out.

"Where is your homework, Brian?" Mr. King asked scornfully.

"Uh, my dog ate it," I said, looking down at my bag.

The class laughed. A quiet burping bark came from my bag, and it wobbled back and forth gently.

"A likely story," Mr. King sneered. "Well, where's your textbook, then?"

"My dog ate that, too," I said, embarrassed.

The class roared with laughter. I could hear a snoozing noise from the bag now.

"Didn't you even come prepared with a pencil?"

"Uh," I mumbled, slumping my head. "Eaten."

I earned detention after school, but it was better than a thwack on the hand with a ruler. Things only went downhill when Mr. King handed out a packet of articles. Seven pages contained all the local events from the past that made national news.

"We're now going to continue our discussion of

how Springs has affected the rest of the world," Mr. King droned.

While the class listened to Mr. King's instructions, I impatiently flipped through the packet. On the very last page a black-and-white picture of Mattie stared up at me. The caption read, "LOCAL GIRL MISS-ING, FEARED DEAD." The article was from 1939.

The three hundred residents of Springs, Long Island, are deeply grieved over the disappearance of twelve-year-old Mattie Bennett. She is feared dead at the hands of a ruthless pirate, although no body has been found. One witness told us that he saw the girl socializing with two strangers wearing over-

alls, when all three were kidnapped by an outlaw and taken into the woods. The man was later caught by a posse of Springs residents as he tried to flee by boat. He had strange writing scrawled on his head, which detectives think may have been a message from one of the children. If you have any information regarding this crime, please contact our offices immediately.

For a moment all the packets in the room disappeared with a flash, only to be replaced by hundreds of the squirming red words "TimeQuest Change." Confused, a few kids blinked and shook their heads. In another flash, all the packets became whole again.

Mattie looked very sad when we were walking home. We tried to convince her that our trip to the future was going to fix everything. Paul even said, "Cheer up, homie." He doesn't call many people "homie," but I guess Mattie didn't know that. Even Video's barking and licking couldn't make her smile. She was homesick in a big way, and I didn't blame her.

When we got home, I knew right away that something was wrong because Dad's car was parked in the driveway. He was supposed to be at work. When we walked inside, Mom was sitting at the kitchen table, looking worried. She stared at Mattie blankly for a moment, but she didn't say anything.

"Go to my room and get ready for our trip," I whispered to Paul and Mattie.

"What's wrong?" I asked Mom after they left.

"Your father's sick, he's red," she said. "Don't disturb him. He's resting in our bedroom, and I've called the ambulance. It's been a strange day. I keep seeing his mother when she was little, roaming around the house."

I stopped breathing just then. Mattie. Dad's mom. Dad, red. I ran up to the master bedroom, where Dad was lying perfectly still. Every few seconds his body disappeared, only to be replaced by thousands of those familiar red words—but this time they read "TimeQuest Error." He flickered back and forth between Dad and the swimming words.

"This … is my last … magic trick," Dad said weakly.

Dad's dresser and mirror flashed red and then disappeared. The red words even replaced the walls, drowning the room in "TimeQuest Error" wallpaper. We had gone against the warning of the TimeQuest comic! By taking Mattie out of the past, I made sure that Dad was never born! I choked back tears for being the worst son imaginable.

"Hang on, Dad, I'm gonna fix everything." I ran to my bedroom. The ambulance blared onto the driveway.

"Your dad's car just turned into a bunch of red words!" Paul announced, peering out the window.

I was afraid Mattie might not want to have kids if she knew she was going to have an orange-haired, comic-collecting, time-traveling killer for a grand-child, but I had to tell the truth. No more lying.

"You're my grandmother, Mattie!" I proclaimed. "So ... Dad's *disappearing!*"

She looked at me with an open mouth.

"Let's go," Paul said.

"Video!" Mattie called. Video peeked out from under the covers and hopped into Mattie's arms.

I stuffed the TimeQuest comic into my pocket alongside the coins, hoping Mattie and Paul wouldn't notice the tears on my face.

"2499 A.D.," I said as clearly as I could, swallowing a sob and pressing the TIMEQUEST button.

We Meet Kelley

A steamy jungle appeared around us. A blond-haired boy floated just above the ground, watching a mutant lizard fight an overgrown ape-man.

"Hey, you're real!" the kid yelled, pressing a remote control. The jungle disappeared, and a shiny black room materialized around us.

"Thank you for using CyberWeb. Have a nice day!" a woman's voice sang.

"Who are you?" I asked, wiping my eyes.

"Are you with the enemy? Are you aliens?" the boy asked, squeezing as far as he could into the corner.

"We're just kids from Springs," I said.

The boy put his hand on his chin and made a thinking noise. Then he typed something into the remote control, and five unfamiliar orange-haired kids appeared in the center of the room, staring blankly. Video ran over to sniff them.

"Inventory of orange-haired children currently residing in the village of East Hampton," a woman's voice sang. The boy clicked the remote again, causing the children to disappear. "Thank you for using

93

CyberWeb. Have a nice day!"

"Did you come to watch the movie?" the boy said, confidently jogging over to us. "Sorry I didn't trust you, but you know, with the war and everything. I'm Kelley."

"It's OK, we really are from Springs," Paul said. "But we time-trav—"

"Look, I just got these," Kelley interrupted, pointing to his feet. When he walked around, the digital words "Kelley Is Great" moved across the sides of his sneakers. "Uh-oh, I hear aliens. Be right back."

Kelley pressed a button on his remote and ran through an opening in the wall. A few minutes later a hatch opened in the ceiling, and he came falling through. Video did an Olympic jump into Mattie's arms.

"Yep, aliens," he continued. "They tried to sell me a mop. You never know with the booby traps around here—one minute I could be mopping, and the next minute, whammo!" He jumped across the room and landed at Paul's feet. "Your sneakers stink," he said to Paul.

We had so many questions for that crazy kid. Who was the enemy? Where were the aliens from? What had happened in the past five hundred years?

"Ugh. History's boring," he answered. "I just got the game Castle Warrior, and you're just the people I need. You can't go in the dungeon unless you have four people."

Kelley made the door reappear, and he led us downstairs to a room containing five spherical pods connected by wires. He pressed a button on his remote, causing the words "VIRTUA POD ACTI-VATION" to appear on the wall. Each pod filled up with a colorful liquid.

"Ready to play?" Kelley asked, climbing the steps of the blue pod. "Hop in!" He dove into the blue liquid.

Confused, I climbed up the steps of the red pod and cautiously lowered myself into the liquid. At once I appeared outside the gate of a spooky castle. A blazing torch stuck out of a brass ring in the wall. Behind me, bats screeched over shadowy trees.

"You're a wizard," Kelley said, adjusting a suit of armor that was much too big for his body.

The purple hat on my head felt real, and the air
smelled like burnt leaves in the fall. I could even taste
my leather armor. The game made me completely
forget about the outside world.

"Pick up that magic spell that's sticking out of the wall," Kelley said.

I picked up a yellow scrap of paper that read, "Fire spell—level one." The paper disappeared as some stars flashed over my head.

"Finally they're here," Kelley cheered, tapping his shiny sword against the gate.

A horse trotted out of the dark forest carrying Mattie and Paul. Mattie wore a suit of black armor. A pointy hat with jingly bells sat on Paul's head.

"Welcome, brave journeyers, to Madame Orph's Castle," a woman's voice boomed from somewhere. "Find the golden key to advance to the next level. Beware, the dragon is hungry, and she does not like to be disturbed. Muahahaha…" The voice trailed off as the front door of the castle creaked open.

"Your sword is bigger than mine," Paul said to Kelley.

"I'm a class A warrior, and you're a class B jester," Kelley answered. "I'll take the lead with the girl. The wizard and the jester have to walk in the back, since they have fewer defensive hit points."

We crept down a dingy hallway filled with cobwebs and scuttling bugs. Kelley handed me a torch and told me to check the floor for traps. I lit up bones of past warriors, bits of dead creatures, and a few gold coins here and there.

When we crept around the first corner, a ghostly scream echoed from the shadows. A glowing skeleton jumped out and attacked Kelley. Its jawbone chattered up and down as it swung a silver scythe. I was too terrified to move.

"Die, beast!" Kelley yelled, swinging his sword.

The skeleton crumbled into a pile of bones on the floor. Rats carried some of them away.

"You could have used your fire spell, y'know," Kelley scoffed at me.

"How am I supposed to do anything with this stick?" Paul complained, scraping his tiny dagger against the wall.

"When that orange-haired kid uses his magic, you'll gain experience points, trust me."

We walked into a large room filled with crumbling pillars. A slithering noise floated out of the darkness. Kelley threw the torch into the middle of the room, revealing a spiked tail curving around the pillars. The thought of its owner sent a chill down my back.

"Show yourself!" Kelley demanded.

Just then the doors closed with a steel clank, leaving us trapped with the slithering thing. We huddled together in the center of the room, each of us facing a different direction.

"Just where I thought I'd find you!" a deep voice cried.

A dragon's head appeared from behind one of the pillars and grabbed Paul. I panicked.

"Use your magic," Kelley reminded me. "Swords are no good against dragons."

I waved my hand, sending a bolt of lightning toward the dragon. It bounced off and sputtered into sparks.

"Only ice works against a dragon, feeble warriors," it laughed. The tail whipped around, cracking pillars

with each swipe. A helpless feeling overcame me as the dragon swallowed Paul and then cried, "DINNER IS SERVED!"

"What are we having?" Kelley asked.

"Chicken and broccoli," the dragon said.

"Can I have my friends over?" Kelley asked, dropping his sword.

"Are they safe?" the dragon inquired, sniffing me and Mattie with big nostrils.

"They're OK, they're from Springs. They just moved here or something."

Just then I appeared back in the pod, floating in the red liquid. Kelley's mom climbed out of a pod labeled "P.I.U.—Parental Interruption Unit."

"You're alive," I said to Paul, relieved that it was all just a waking dream. Paul looked shaken up.

After dinner Kelley invited us to sleep over. We floated on invisible hover beds. The CyberWeb turned Kelley's room into outer space, and we soared past planets and stars.

"We're from the year 2001," I said, showing Kelley my TimeQuest ring.

"Wow, I haven't been visited for a long time," he answered. "My last TimeQuest visitor came from 99,999 A.D. to learn about the war."

"Who are you fighting?" Mattie asked.

"East Hampton and aliens," Kelley said. "See, in 2451 aliens attacked Earth, but they lost the battle and went into hiding. Then in 2469 a hurricane washed away all the East Hampton beaches, and the war started when East Hamptonites invaded Springs to steal sand. Everybody thinks they're working with the aliens to drive the people from Springs off their land."

"That's awful!" I moaned. East Hampton was always the only place where Springs kids could go to the movies. Now there was officially nothing to do around here!

"We're in a truce now," Kelley said. "But they don't last long."

The TimeQuest ring glowed red all night, but these clues gave us enough to whisper about after Kelley fell asleep.

"Don't you see, if we go far enough into the future, we'll be able to get another TimeQuest comic," I said. "There are more of them. They haven't been invented yet."

"The time traveler who visited Kelley must be from a time after they've been invented," Paul added.

"How did Mr. Somerset get one, then?" Mattie asked.

"Beats me," I said. "Maybe he really does have super powers. If we get one, you can probably use it to get home, Mattie. I bet a new TimeQuest ring lets you start over and go anywhere."

"Did you hear that, Video? We might get home," Mattie said happily. Video snored.

"What about *Superman?*" Paul asked.

"It's gone," I said. "We don't know what year to

warp to in prehistoric times, and that was Mr. Somerset's last one."

"But if we get another TimeQuest comic, we can warp to before we warped back to Mr. Somerset," Paul explained. "Then we can get a whole bunch of *Superman #1*'s."

"Yeah, and maybe destroy the world," I said. My head spun trying to think about it. "My dad's already disappearing back home. Let's just drop it."

"But that's the whole reason—"

"Every time I get near *Superman #1* disaster strikes. Let's just forget it. I can deal."

Later that night, memories of Dad storming into my room haunted me. A dark shadow stood next to me, screaming, "How could you? This was my most valuable possession! I was going to retire off this comic! Now I'll have to work until I die!" He slammed the door on the way out, leaving a dent in the doorframe that still exists today.

As bad as it felt to be thinking about IT, replacing *Superman #1* seemed silly compared to getting Mattie home and fixing Dad. I cried myself to sleep, tortured by a dreadful despair.

We Go
to School

I slept comfortably on the hover bed, but I couldn't figure out how to get down in the morning. I sat on the edge, staring hopelessly down at the floor far below.

"Time for school," Kelley's mom said brightly, peeking into the room.

"I don't want to go to school," we whined simultaneously.

The beds dropped suddenly, and we fell to the floor in a heap.

"Mommm! Did you have to program the beds to do that?" Kelley complained.

The TimeQuest ring was glowing red, so we knew we'd have to go to school with Kelley. He took a long time programming the color of his outfit and the phrase on his sneakers. After a while, he forgot about school altogether and turned on the CyberWeb. A man dropped out of the ceiling and tapped Kelley on the shoulder, saying, "Sorry, time to learn."

Eventually we walked to school. The General Store, the church, the school, and the meeting hall were now shiny black rectangles. Electronic ducks with red eyes waddled around Parson's Pond. A digital sign read, "Do not oil the ducks!"

"I think we're late," Kelley said, pressing the button on his remote. A hatch opened in the side of the school.

"I've been going to school for almost six hundred years," Paul complained.

A screen in the lobby read, "END THE WAR WITH EAST HAMPTON FOR GOOD! SAVE THE CHILDREN!" A big red heart hovered between "Springs" and "East Hampton."

Kelley led us to a classroom, where we peeked in the window of the door. A woman with spiked hair politely told the class to take attendance. At once the students rubbed their thumbs over little white squares on their desks. A lady's voice came out of the ceiling, singing, "Nancy ... present ... Timmy ... present ... Billy ... present ..." and so on. After the room became quiet, the teacher programmed an assignment onto the computerized blackboard.

Kelley creaked the classroom door open, and we crept toward an empty row of desks. Everything went well until Kelley swiped his hand over the attendance square. He tried to move his hand slowly, whispering "Shhh" to his thumb. It was no use. A loud beep sounded, and the female computer voice sang, "Kelley is *tardy!*"

"Kelley, that's the third time this month," the

teacher reprimanded, her green eyes glowing. "Once more and you lose all virtual-reality privileges."

"Sorry, Mrs. Q," Kelley groaned, drooping his head.

Kelley didn't get punished at all. Mrs. Q didn't whack him with a ruler or give him detention. I swiped my thumb over the little white square on my desk. A loud siren blared.

"INTRUDER ALERT! INTRUDER ALERT!" a deep voice shouted from the ceiling. A metallic orb slowly descended out of a hatch near the front of the room. It whirred back and forth between me, Paul, and Mattie. Video barked at it.

"POSSIBLE EAST HAMPTON INVASION!" the voice boomed. "INTRUDERS, LEAVE THE CLASSROOM IMMEDIATELY! YOU HAVE TEN SECONDS TO COMPLY!"

"Class, assume defense position!" Mrs. Q ordered. The whole class dove under their desks and put their heads between their knees. Video howled as Mrs. Q picked up an electronic yardstick and waved it at us, yelling, "Stay back!" I was too confused to run anywhere, and Paul and Mattie sat frozen.

"YOU HAVE FAILED TO COMPLY," the thundering voice continued. "YOU WILL NOW BE VAPORIZED!"

Zwing! Zwing! The orb flashed purple beams around the room.

"You guys should, uh, probably go," Kelley said calmly.

Paul, Mattie, and I scrambled for the door while the whole class screamed from beneath the desks. When we entered the hallway, three large guards wearing orange uniforms snatched us up. A fourth went back into the room for Kelley. As they dragged us away, the female voice sang, "Invasion terminated. Learning will commence in thirty seconds …"

Kelley had a lot of explaining to do in the principal's office. The principal was a large man with red cheeks, who seemed much more interested in pulling pieces of candy out of his drawer than anything else. Menacing guards stood on both sides of him.

"You caused a lot of trouble in class today, student 13579," the principal said. He threw a piece of candy in the air. It exploded like a firecracker, and the principal opened his mouth to catch some of it with his tongue.

"You should have told me you were going to launch a Sugar Zapper," Kelley said. "I would've opened my mouth. By the way, you can call me Kelley."

"Student 13579," the principal continued, "you have violated section 946a of the Springs School Student Code of Expectations. 'Students shall not bring guests to class without first registering them in the main office.' We *must* be careful during this time of war." He tried to get his hand unstuck from the code booklet. "This would normally call for suspension."

"They're not from East Hampton," Kelley whined. "Be a pal, I want to go on the field trip today."

"I looked up your guests on the CyberWeb," the principal continued, looking at me suspiciously. "I am certain they are not spies."

"Told ya!" Kelley bragged. "You owe me a Coke!" He hopped onto the principal's desk and fiddled with a toy. The guards reached over to grab Kelley.

"Let him be," the principal ordered. He tugged at the skin hanging from his chin, as if he might pull it off at any moment. "Seeing as this is your first offense, I'm willing to let you go with a warning."

"You're good," Kelley said, pointing at him approvingly.

"Just remember that during the next principal's election," he demanded, unwrapping a large piece of candy labeled "Zappers!"

"Open your mouths," Kelley directed as the principal pressed a button on the candy.

I jumped under a chair. I wasn't about to try a piece of exploding candy offered by a school principal.

"Cherry Zapper!" the principal signaled, tossing the candy into the air.

A red blast filled the room. Kelley caught a chunk of red sugar in his mouth. A big red lump landed in my hair and melted into an annoying ooze.

We Go on a Very, Very Interesting Field Trip

After Kelley got us out of trouble, the principal said that we could go on the field trip. The TimeQuest ring was still glowing red, so we decided to join the rest of the class to see an archaeological exhibit at the meeting hall.

An electronic sign outside the hall read:

TREASURES OF THE MUD PITS
A local archaeological exhibit sponsored by the Springs Historical Society

A big crowd was gathered by the entrance, where a flock of guards wearing sunglasses searched bags and checked identification. Kelley explained to a guard that we were OK, even though we didn't show up in the records. The guard became suspicious when Mrs. Q and the rest of the class wouldn't come anywhere near us.

"Sorry," the guard said, pushing us away from the crowd. "No unauthorized personnel allowed."

"Go around to the back," Kelley whispered before disappearing into the meeting hall.

We walked around the building and stood by a slick black wall, wondering what Kelley was up to. Then a door whizzed open, and Kelley waved us in.

"I can talk my way into the White House," Kelley said, playing with a yo-yo. "This is the door to the archaeologist's room."

We walked past piles of fossilized bones and half-built creatures. Kelley high-fived a guard, and we came out into a large room crowded with people. A skinny man with curly brown hair ran around to a bunch of exhibits covered by white sheets, peeking under each one.

"That's Professor Henderson, the town archaeologist," Kelley whispered.

"Welcome, ladies and gentlemen and students of Springs," the announcer blared. "We are very proud of the exhibits here today. They represent the efforts of dozens of archaeologists working over the past fifty years. As you may or may not know, the ancient Springs mud pits were discovered in 2449 by a small boy digging in a stream …"

Paul leaned over to me and said, "You're flickering."

I looked down at myself, only to see that thousands of the red words "TimeQuest Error" formed my body. The words squirmed around like frenzied insects until my body reappeared. I looked desperately at Paul for help, but he seemed just as horrified as I was.

"The first display item is an ancient fossilized mastodon!" the announcer said as I flickered rapidly between myself and the red words.

Professor Henderson pulled the sheet off one of the mounds, revealing a giant skeleton with tusks stretched high in the air.

"The mastodon likely came to North America across a land bridge formed during the ice ages …"

Suddenly the TimeQuest ring beeped, and to my relief the words "Protagonist Rescue Algorithm commencing …" scrolled across the digital display. My flickering slowed down.

"And now, ladies and gentlemen—the dire wolf!"

Professor Henderson pulled the sheet off another mound, revealing a huge skeleton of a dire wolf snarling at the crowd.

"Imagine coming face to face with this giant predator," the announcer said. A few children held on to their parents in fear.

"Bor-ing," I said to Paul, eyeing my TimeQuest ring's digital display, which busily flashed a series of cryptic signs and symbols. I found the ring's super-advanced technology comforting.

After presenting a giant sloth and a bunch of other exhibits, the archaeologist stood next to two small white mounds.

"We can't explain this strange artifact, so I'm just going to ask you to let your imaginations run wild," the announcer admitted. "Inside an encrustation of seashells and fossilized seaweed, we discovered this. Professor Henderson, if you will!"

The archaeologist pulled back the white sheet from one of the small mounds, revealing …

... *Superman #1* sitting inside of its protective case!

My heart skipped a beat. I blinked my eyes a few times to make sure it was real.

"That's right, folks, a comic book. It was lost over twelve thousand years *before* comic books were invented. Since we found it buried in an untouched geological deposit, there can be no mistaking it. We are dealing with some sort of supernatural force here."

"Does this mean the rumors about time travel are true?" a member of the crowd interrupted.

"Hey, I've been visited," another crowd member added.

"Neither Professor Henderson nor I know the answer to this riddle," the announcer continued. "We were given only one clue: a tiny hair stuck inside the plastic case. We carefully removed it and reconstructed a picture of its owner through DNA Fibrial Reconstructive Engineering. We tried to re-create the facial expression that this creature might have had if it found itself stuck in the mud pits alongside these prehistoric creatures."

Paul and I looked at each other with wide eyes.

"Professor Henderson! The final exhibit, if you will!"

The archaeologist pulled the cover off the last exhibit, revealing a giant picture of my face. It showed my mouth wide open under surprised eyes. Video hopped out of Mattie's arms to get a closer look while the crowd just stared at it, utterly quiet.

At that moment a nearby girl noticed me flickering. She looked at me, then back at the picture, then back at me. Suddenly she let out a high-pitched scream. The presentation stopped, and everybody turned in my direction. A mother grabbed her children and ran for the door, crying, "The aliens are here!" Men fought each other to get out of the building. Cries of "We're under attack!" and "The truce has been broken!" filled the room.

The archaeologist tried desperately to protect the exhibits from a stampeding mob. It was hopeless. The dire wolf crashed to the ground in a tumble of bones, and the mastodon collapsed onto its tusks. The giant sloth dove onto *Superman #1*, and they both disappeared in a pile of rubble. The only object still standing was the giant picture of my face, which looked surprised while everybody fled in panic.

Before I could get anywhere, a guard grabbed me and said, "You're coming with me, alien!" Another guard grabbed Mattie and Paul. They dragged us outside and confiscated everything we had, including the TimeQuest comic, my ring, and all four TimeQuest coins. Kelley tried to talk the guards out of taking us, but his charm was no match for the cruelty of those men. They threw us on the ground and tied us up. I hoped to flicker away before their eyes, just to show them that I could escape their evil grasp.

We Meet the Professor, and Then…

As the sun beat down on us from above, the gentle lapping of the bullfrogs in the pond announced a somewhat indefatigable ennui circulating in the noonday air; no doubt, an ennui characterized by the oppressive beating of the sun and an incessant lapping of bullfrogs; forsooth!

OK, maybe I won't narrate old-fashioned style.

We were trapped, and it was hot.

Professor Henderson came over to us wearing a stern expression. His leg bones pushed out big blue veins, which twitched as he walked. He stopped nearby and stared at us in our helpless position.

"Why, why, why?" he whined, hopping up and down so that both feet hit the ground at the same time.

"It was an accident. We're not aliens," I assured him, relieved that I flickered only once in a while now.

"No, the death of the dinosaurs was an accident," he said. "This was treachery!" Then he pulled his hair and paced back and forth, saying, "I am not getting upset, the little birdie told me not to get upset …"

"Shall I lock them up?" one of the guards asked.

"Not yet," the professor said, pointing to me. "This one intrigues me. He looks exactly like the boy in that picture."

Kelley walked up to Professor Henderson and explained that this was all the result of an innocent practical joke, and that we had just dropped the comic book in the archaeological dig for fun.

The professor said incredulously, "Are you going to stand there and tell me that you reconstructed thirteen thousand years' worth of fossilized seaweed on the outside of that plastic case, and then embedded the comic inside an ancient layer of alluvial limestone under three tons of sedimentary rock?"

"Uh, yeah," Kelley answered, digging nervously at the ground with his foot.

"Then how do you explain these items?" he asked, holding out the TimeQuest ring and coins. The ring glowed green.

"We got them in a cereal box," Kelley said. "They were a prize."

"Lock them away," the professor ordered calmly, holding his hands over his ears. "All of them."

The guards cast shadows over us.

"Wait! I'll tell you the truth," I shouted. "We went back in time to get a comic book using that ring, but we got stuck in prehistoric Springs. We lost the comic in a swamp there."

"Uh, see, I told ya!" Kelley said, anxiously doing tricks with his yo-yo.

"So, the rumors are true," Professor Henderson chortled, jingling the objects in front of me again. "I was right about the ring. Guards, untie them!"

Before another word was spoken, Video howled angrily from inside the meeting hall.

"A prehistoric beast?" the professor asked, coughing. "You brought one back? Tell me, what? A sloth?"

"Kind of," I said.

We walked into the meeting hall and trudged through the rubble of the ruined exhibit. At Professor Henderson's command, the guards waited at the door.

When we found Video, he was snarling at a large computer monitor that had folded out of the wall. The screen showed a green alien with bulging eyes sitting on a floating throne. The creature wore a jeweled robe, and a ring of gold spikes surrounded its face.

"My slaves, the time has come to return," the alien announced, pressing a button with one of its six arms. A loud pinging noise began immediately, and the meeting hall began to vibrate. Control panels folded out of the wall, chairs rose from the floor, and large windows opened up all around us. A row of video screens descended from the ceiling, each one displaying an incomprehensible series of statistics and pictures. When the vibrating stopped, we were standing in the cockpit of a spaceship!

"The aliens!" Professor Henderson yelled. He made a frantic dash out the doorway, dropping the TimeQuest items on the ground outside.

"Let's get out of here!" Paul said, pulling me toward the door. Mattie grabbed Video, and we sprinted for the exit. On the way, my foot got caught in the jawbone of the giant sloth, and I fell into the pile of fossils.

"Come on," Paul urged from outside.

I freed my foot from the sloth and stumbled toward the door, but Mrs. Q and the chubby principal materialized in front of it and blocked my way.

"At last the Supreme Commander has summoned us," the principal said, tearing off some of the loose skin under his chin.

"Yes, I have awaited the pinging beacon for decades," Mrs. Q added, her eyes glowing green.

"I became certain you were a colonist when you did not show up in the Earthlings' CyberWeb," the principal declared, grabbing my hand. "I don't know how you existed so long here without a forged identity, but all colonists must leave now to be replaced by a fresh group." The building shook as an explosive blast went off underneath me.

"But I *am* an Earthling!" I cried, trying to pull myself away from the principal. More green-eyed

Springs villagers appeared at the door, discussing the Supreme Commander.

"Children forget so easily," Mrs. Q said. "Perhaps if we all return to our normal form, it will remind you of your homeland. Computer, remove pseudo-layer now!"

A purple haze filled the room momentarily, causing all the clothes and skin of the aliens to fall off. When the light returned to normal, slimy green aliens with bulging eyes stood around me. They appeared concerned that I did not look like them. The six-armed principal tried to strap me into a chair, but I fought hard.

"Computer, complete the transformation!" Mrs. Q continued, staring at me fretfully.

A pink haze filled the room, causing all the aliens to hunch over and shrink. The furniture and computer devices shrank along with them. Now a pack of two-foot-high mutants surrounded me! Slime dripped from their sharp teeth, and retractable claws appeared at the end of each arm.

"Namuh era uoy!" the principal squeaked, shaking a tiny fist at me. He kicked me, but I barely felt it. I picked him up and tossed him across the room, where he landed in a pile of fossils.

"Mih teg!" the principal squealed as the spaceship slowly lifted off the ground.

I ran desperately toward the closing cabin door, but the pack of mutants leaped at me and clamped their claws onto my pants. I dangled over the ground as Paul and Mattie screamed, "Hurry!"

When Video saw what was happening, he climbed onto Mattie's shoulders and said, "Groff frowf *garfff!*"

At once the mutants whimpered and let go of my pants. I fell past the blazing engine fire and squished into the mud next to Parson's Pond.

The spaceship soared toward the clouds. Just before leaving the atmosphere, it stopped, and a mess of debris rained from the cabin door. A few seconds later the ship disappeared in a bright blue flash, and fossils glooped into the mud around me.

Superman #1 crashed next to me, as if to say, "I'm back!" The plastic case was beat up and scuffed, but

the comic was still in mint condition. Even the hair was gone now! I looked down at my pants. They were still there, and the corduroy hadn't even been torn!

"The war is back!" Kelley announced, watching the Springs army march down the street. "They don't let us kids fight, though."

Fortunately we found the TimeQuest comic, the ring, and two of the coins in the grass where the professor had dropped them. I handed the coins to Mattie and Paul, slipped the ring onto my finger, and held both comics tightly.

"What year do I tell it, guys?" I asked.

"99,999 A.D.," Paul said. Immediately that year appeared on the digital display.

"Bye, Kelley, thanks for everything," I said, pressing the TIMEQUEST button.

"Good luck in the war," Mattie added, hugging Video tightly.

Kelley waved while he looked around for his yo-yo. An explosion sounded in the distance, and then …

We Meet Nathan

We found ourselves on a windswept beach next to a raging ocean. Tremendous waves crashed back and forth, sending sea spray high into the air. Black clouds threw bolts of lightning into the gurgling soup, and the roaring wind made the trees beg for mercy. Out of the mist, a wave as high as the sky curled toward us.

"Over here!" Paul cried through the howling wind. He stood on a metal platform and fiddled with some green buttons on a pole.

I followed two shadowy figures as they scrambled over to the platform. Video fought the wind and crawled into Mattie's overalls. As the wave threw a shadow over us, the platform lowered into the ground, and a metal ceiling slid overhead. We descended into the blackness of the Earth. The only light came from my green TimeQuest ring and a bouncing yellow circle.

I held my comic tightly. Perhaps *Superman #1* wasn't worth the trouble it had caused, but it gave me hope that things could be perfect again. Distant times may have extreme video games, rare comic books, and programmable clothing, but the only really cool place is where people actually care whether you're swallowed by giant waves or kidnapped by aliens. I finally understood why Mattie and Mikey were so happy with their primitive toys—they were home.

Suddenly the lights came on with a clank. A door slid open, revealing a huge underground cavern. Long icicles of rock sent droplets toward the sandy floor. A sign read, "Welcome to Springs." Springs now sat far underground, and the elevator had taken us away from the hostile surface. Kelley stood in front of me, happily playing with a glowing yo-yo.

"I found my yo-yo," Kelley said through a popping

bubble. "It was under this coin that says TimeQuest."

"Crudmuffins." I was definitely under an evil spell, one that brought me something bad every time I had *Superman #1* in my possession. Now Kelley was stuck with us too!

Our feet carved long lines in the sand as we trudged through the monstrous cavern. Chattering bugs burrowed around us, pecking away at our sneakers whenever we stopped. Meanwhile, my TimeQuest ring continued to flash mathematical equations and complicated computer code. I didn't understand any of it, but that was OK. All I cared about was that I had stopped flickering entirely.

"I don't know if we did this right," Paul said after a while, looking around at the emptiness.

"Let's see," I answered, opening the TimeQuest comic.

I found the panel that read, "But wait, what's this? ..." The next panel showed Dad flickering in bed while I stood over him. The caption read, "Despite grave warnings, our adventurers have meddled with the space-time continuum, tragically altering the past and the future. Will our heroes prevent Brian's dad from flickering away?"

Our adventures with Kelley filled the next panels. I fell out of the spaceship in a two-page drawing, while a bubble with the word "Yeaaaagghhh!" came out of my mouth.

An ad on the next page showed a kid carrying a copy of *TimeQuest 2: The Revenge of Physics*.

Your adventure is almost over!
But there's more in store from
TimeQuest Incorporated ...
Are you tired of warping back to the present
only to find that life has unpredictably changed?
Well, TimeQuest Incorporated
is proud to announce ...

TimeQuest 2: The Revenge of Physics
will be available soon
at a TimeQuest store near you!

New features include:
1. A <u>setting</u> for how you would like space-time continuum changes to occur: Gradual,

Instantaneous, Partial, or dozens of other ways!

2. An UNDO feature to correct terrible mistakes (patent pending).

3. A NO CHANGE option, to avoid changes altogether. Using Quantum Mechanical algorithms, our physicists now have the ability to create alternate universes for your touring pleasure. This prevents changing the future of our universe altogether!

4. You can now warp to within fifty years of any previous warp time!

For the low price of only 10 purple coins!

The words "Copyright 99,999" appeared in very tiny letters at the bottom of the page.

"We warped to the right time!" Mattie cheered.

Just then a droning voice filled the cavern. "I—am—Nathan … I—am—Nathan … I—am—Nathan …" A boy wandered toward us from the distance, saying the words over and over. When he finally reached us, he adjusted his thick glasses and said, "I—am—Nathan."

"Are you a robot?" Kelley asked.

"Try some programmable gum," Nathan said, handing out silver-wrapped packs of gum. "My favorite flavor is Swizzle Fizz, that's the swixiest. I—am—Nathan. I'm not a robot. It just sounds deranged to talk like this."

"I don't know," I said, sniffing the gum. "Candy and I just don't mix."

"It's all computerized," he said, showing us a portable keyboard. "Just type in the flavor you want."

I carefully typed in G-R-A-P-E, but Video hopped onto the keyboard, creating the flavor G-R-A-P-E-Q-A-S-Z-X. My gum tasted like metal, and I swore off candy forever.

Suddenly my ring beeped, and a new message scrolled across the digital display: "Sorry! Backup processor insufficient to complete Protagonist Rescue Algorithm." The ring glowed yellow for a few seconds and then changed back to green.

"Oh no!" I wailed as a swarm of the red words "TimeQuest Error" replaced my body.

"You're flickering," Nathan said to me. "It's the TimeQuest curse. Everybody's had some problem. The company came out with the new version because of all the lawsuits. I lost my allowance this week because I made my mom's HargleBeast flicker away. Isn't this gum drax?"

"Nathan, can you help us get more TimeQuest comics so we can fix things?" Paul asked, looking at me worriedly.

"Yes, but hurry," Nathan answered, beckoning us to follow him. "Tonight is New Year's Eve, according to the Dranex-II calendar, and the emperor wants to set off underground fireworks to welcome the year 100,000. I had a bad dream last night that the whole world collapsed after the fireworks. Most humans are leaving Earth. My parents are waiting for me in the Honey Way galaxy, but I told them I have to save the world first. What year are you from?"

"1939."

"2001."

"2499."

"Wow," Nathan said. "2499 was the year that the truce was broken in the Springs–East Hampton War. I got that right on a test yesterday."

"Who won the war?" Kelley asked. Then he drooped his head and said, "What happened to my mom?"

"East Hampton surrendered in 2579, and a peace treaty was signed that same year. The agreement lasted until 77,340, when the Great Orbital Shift changed everything. Then East Hampton and Springs had to go underground because the surface turned violent, and nobody cared about the beaches anymore. I wrote an essay on it."

Our journey took us through dozens of underground caves and elevators. Nathan showed us different "zones" that existed all over the world, accessible only by teleportation chambers. We went to the CandyWarp Zone, the Adventure Zone, and the Emotion Zone. Kelley wanted to go back to the CandyWarp Zone a second time, but he changed his mind when I reminded him that I might disappear.

Nathan Takes Us Shopping

We eventually teleported to the Shopping Zone, where crowds of alien tourists milled in and out of colorful stores. The creatures had three eyes surrounded by spikes, or long trunks that dripped slimy liquid, or bodies turned inside out.

"If I'm reading your mind right, you're thinking about home," Nathan said to me. "Why do you think your dad doesn't like you?"

"Twenty minutes until the centimillennial fireworks!" a voice boomed from above.

"We haven't got much time," Nathan observed, peering up at the ceiling. "This week I deposited ten TimeQuest comics in different time periods, hoping somebody from the past would come here and see what terrible thing is going to happen tonight. Maybe they could try to change something. You're the only ones that came."

We walked into the TimeQuest Outlet. A sign read, "*TimeQuest 2: The Revenge of Physics* will be available immediately after the centimillennial fireworks!" A storekeeper was preparing the TimeQuest 2 display.

He had a single bushy eyebrow spanning both eyes.

"We need two TimeQuest comics fast," Nathan said.

The shopkeeper glanced at us halfheartedly and then continued to prepare the display case.

"Four purple coins," he said coldly. "I see you made short work of the last ten you bought," he added, looking at Nathan.

"I forgot, I spent my last purple on this pack of gum," Nathan said to us, shrugging his shoulders. "And I left my hypno ring back in my Base Zone."

"Please, sir, my grandson is disappearing," Mattie said, holding out my flickering arm. "I have to get back home."

The man stood up and retrieved a brown box from a nearby shelf. He opened it and dumped out dozens of used TimeQuest comics at our feet.

"Read them if you want," the man said. "They all end the same way—with blank panels." He picked up a few of the comics and flipped through them. "See this one? These girls were having a fabulous time in ancient Egypt until they chipped off a piece of the Sphinx as a souvenir. And this one? Two brothers went back to Spain in 1492 and gave Columbus a map. And here, this boy showed our ancestors how to put roller skate wheels in a row instead of side by side. It all seemed harmless until they warped home and found that everything had changed." He tossed the comics back into the pile.

"But this was an accident," I said.

"They all say that," the shopkeeper sneered. "I've watched dozens of children flicker away before my eyes while they're begging me to fix their messes." He grabbed my TimeQuest comic and flipped through it. "Ah, yes, exciting. Snot, dire wolves, aliens. A fine adventure. I'm impressed."

"So you'll give us the comics?" I asked nervously, worried that my TimeQuest comic would end up in the box with all the others.

"Kids don't know the meaning of responsibility these days. If I give you two comics now, you'll come back begging for four later, saying you have to save the world or something."

"But we *do* have to save the world," Nathan argued.

"And I used to have two normal eyebrows!" the shopkeeper snapped, pointing to his shaggy uni-brow. "Until last month when some kids meddled with the past, trying to save the world! Well, the world's still here, but now I'm stuck with this hairy monstrosity! Get out of here before I sic my HargleBeast on you, and don't come back until you have the coins!"

Disheartened, we trudged through the busy mall. Every few seconds my body disappeared, replaced with the wildly bouncing words "Terminal TimeQuest Error." A few aliens looked at me curiously. I was terrified by the idea of not existing anywhere in the universe.

When we came to a store called the Yo-Yo Emporium, Kelley dragged us inside. A woman in a sparkling white dress walked over to us and smiled.

"Welcome to the Yo-Yo Emporium. We stock the finest quality yo-yos from all regions, planets, and eras. We also carry just yos. Please, take your time, look around. My name is Yo-Yo Flo, but you can call me Yo!"

"'Sup, Yo?" Paul said.

At once Yo spotted Kelley's yellow yo-yo. "Is that what I think it is?" she asked. "Could that be a Spin-O-Matic Xj5000 glow-in-the-dark yo-yo from the Springs War era?"

"Yeah," Paul said. "Do you want to buy it?"

Kelley protested, but Paul yanked the yo-yo away from him, saying, "My best friend is disappearing. I think you can spare a yo-yo."

I had never heard Paul call me anything other than a "homie" before, so it was nice to hear him say such a cool thing about me. He can be serious sometimes, but he usually just jokes around. Anyway, I don't know if it's a coincidence, but right after he said it, everything around me turned into ghostly shadows. My limbs felt weak, and I lay down on the floor. That's the last thing I remember, so Paul's going to narrate this part …

Hey. It's Paul. Word. I tried to erase that corny part where I called Brian my best friend and he fainted. Ow, he just hit me with a pillow. All right, I'll tell the story. Once upon a time, in a dark forest, lived an orange-haired boy named Brian. He liked porridge. Ow.

Yo-Yo Flo said that only a few hundred Xj5000s were ever made because the company started making grenades after the Springs–East Hampton War started. She bought it for one purple coin. It wasn't enough money to buy a TimeQuest comic, so we begged her for more.

"Sorry," Yo-Yo Flo said. "But my cousin Yertle might be interested in buying some of the vintage clothing that you're wearing."

We carried Brian over to a store called Yertle's Antique Clothing.

"Can that be a pre-Alien War pair of corduroy pants?" the woman swooned, walking over to Brian's flickering body. She wore an antique dress that looked like a parachute.

"Yeah, you want to buy them?" I asked. Ow.

"I'll give you two purples and a green for them," she offered, holding a magnifying glass up to Brian's leg. "They're a bit flickery but remarkably well preserved."

"Three purple coins, and I'll throw in the belt," I bargained.

"Deal!"

"Five minutes until the centimillennial fireworks," the voice announced.

We carried Brian back to the TimeQuest Outlet and bought two TimeQuest comics with our money.

"If you warp from here, you'll end up in the middle of the ground back home," Nathan warned. "Follow me."

We rode one of the elevators up to the violent surface. We huddled together on the metal platform and set our TimeQuest rings as thunder boomed all around us.

"One minute until the centimillennial fireworks," the voice rumbled from below.

"Tell Brian I said good-bye," Mattie said, putting a coin in Video's mouth. "I had a swell time, but I miss my family."

Video said, "Yip," and blinked his eye. I think he

swallowed the coin. Mattie pressed her ring and disappeared.

As I showed Kelley how to use the comic, the first firework went off underneath us, causing the ground around the platform to crumble away.

"In 1970 I hypnotized your General Store owner to give a TimeQuest comic away when someone said, 'I had a bad dream last night,'" Nathan explained. "People who have bad dreams *want* to change things, so I'm counting on you to save our world." Without another word, Nathan pressed a button on his clothing and disappeared.

Another firework exploded under us, and water from the surface poured into the cavern. Suddenly, flames shot up all around us, and the metal platform swayed slowly back and forth.

"See ya!" Kelley said, waving. "Come back if you wanna play Virtua Pod. I'm getting Death Fighter next week when it comes out." He pressed the button on his ring and disappeared.

When a firework detonated above us, the rest of the ground as far as I could see collapsed into the underground cavern. The ocean fell away, creating a boom that popped my ears. Just before the splash devoured the platform, I leaned over and pressed the HOME button on Brian's ring. That's all. I guess Brian will tell you the rest. Peace out, reader homies.

I Tell You About the Resolution

The next thing I remembered was waking up in my bedroom wearing my Superman boxer shorts. Paul looked at me in a concerned way until I stopped flickering. All of my strength came back to me pretty quickly. I stood up and walked over to the window, just in time to see the ambulance speed away carrying Mom and Dad. After all, it was still Tuesday afternoon, only a few seconds after we left for the future.

"Your dad will go back to normal now," Paul said, leaning on the windowsill. "Mattie's back home."

"I don't know. The TimeQuest comic is so unreliable," I said. "But I guess Mattie made it home OK, since I'm whole again."

Suddenly there was a red flash from beside my window.

"Hey, check it out!" Paul said, pointing to tiny writing scratched on the inside of my window frame.

Dear Brian,

I made it back home OK. Nathan was good at getting us to the right spot. I appeared right in my backyard! I had a swell time with you on our adventure. It will be something to tell our grandchildren about. Oops, you already know all about it. Anyway, all that danger turned me off comic collecting. I'm going to throw out all of my comic books and start collecting baseball cards. Bye!

—Mattie

"I can't believe we did it," Paul said, holding *Superman #1* like a baby. "The comic's awesome! I have to go home and wrestle my brother again, though. It's been too long."

Before I knew it, I was all by myself. I snuck down to the den and placed *Superman #1* on Dad's desk,

right next to a pile of shiny paper showing baby ducks chewing pacifiers. I sprinted out and waited by the front door for Mom and Dad to come home, imagining how happy Dad would be when he saw the comic.

"You don't ever have to go to school again," Dad said, waving Superman #1.

Finally the taxi pulled up, and Mom and Dad walked in.

"We're back," Mom said. "It was a false alarm."

"The doctor said it was probably just gas," Dad continued.

"I'll never give your dad my leftover stew for lunch again," Mom promised.

Dad smiled and walked into the den. I felt like jumping around. After five long years of worry, things were about to go back to normal. Dad would never have to secretly hate me again.

I didn't take a breath the whole time he was in the den. When he came out, he patted me on the back and said, "We celebrate this weekend. Do you want to go to the amusement park on Saturday? We'll take a trip to Great Adventure. You can ask Paul to come."

He didn't say anything about *Superman #1*, but I didn't really care. I knew he had seen it.

Everything was great for the rest of the week—well, except when my mom asked where all my pants were. It was time for the truth again.

"Mom, Paul and I had the best adventure, but I lost

all my pants. We got this comic called TimeQuest at the General Store, and then we warped back to 75 million B.C., and a sea monster ate my jeans. Then we warped to 1939 to get a copy of *Superman #1*, and we met Mattie and her mutant one-eyed dog and got kidnapped by an outlaw and accidentally warped to prehistoric times, and I got into a fight with a mastodon and dropped the comic. Then my overalls fell off, and we warped home, and then Dad started disappearing, so we warped to the future and met Kelley. He showed us a cool video game, and then we went to school and almost got vaporized, but Kelley talked our way out of it. Then we went on a field trip and almost got kid-

napped by aliens! I got *Superman #1* back, though, and then we warped into the way future and met a smart kid named Nathan. He gave us programmable gum and took us to get more TimeQuest comics. Paul sold Kelley's yo-yo and my corduroys for four purple coins, and then we bought some comics and warped home right before I disappeared into oblivion."

"Oh, that's nice," Mom said as she folded laundry. She even forgot about my missing pants.

I had an incredible week. Really, it was the best. When Dad joked around with me, I didn't worry anymore that he was just pretending to like me. We played foam basketball one day, and another day he made a portrait of me in his oatmeal with syrup. He also showed me how to make a whole roll of toilet paper disappear with his magic.

My biggest problem all week was when Paul and I couldn't decide what order we were going to ride the big roller coasters. Paul slept over Friday night, and when Saturday came around we were up at the crack of dawn. While waiting for Mom and Dad to get up, we crept into the den to see if we could find *Superman #1*. We just had to look at it one last time.

We made a terrible discovery. The ultimate protective case for *Superman #1* lay empty on Dad's desk.

"What's this?" Paul asked, fiddling with the small glass dome where Dad usually kept the wrecked comic.

The dome now contained a half-eaten baseball card.

Mom walked in wearing a nightgown and said, "I thought I heard something scurrying around in here."

"Mom, why is there a baseball card under this glass dome?" I asked. "What's going on?" I couldn't bring myself to ask where the mint-condition *Superman #1* was.

"Oh, you already know that story, Brian," Mom said. "Grandma Matilda used to collect baseball cards. She saved a special one for Dad, a Honus Wagner card from 1909 in mint condition, worth a million dollars. One day when you were four, you were sitting on the bed with Dad while he dusted it. While he was leaning over to get a new plastic case from under the bed, you picked up the card and put it in your mouth. When Dad looked up again, you said, 'Honuth Wagnah, Honuth Wagnah.' He tried desperately to pull the card from your mouth, but only half of it came out."

I didn't remember anything like that happening! I still remembered the comic book accident as clearly as if it had happened yesterday. Suddenly the baseball card flickered into the red words "TimeQuest Change." Before Mom even noticed, the words turned back into the half-eaten card.

Just then Dad walked into the den and stumbled over to his desk, looking groggy. He pushed aside the empty plastic case and picked up a present wrapped in colorful paper with little pictures of Superman all over it. I noticed the cover price of ten cents, the crease where the spine was, the dark handwriting filling the comic panels. I fell to my knees. The words "64 pages of action" and "All in full color" flashed before my eyes. I was going to throw up.

"Happy birthday," he said, handing me the present. "We'll set out for Great Adventure after breakfast, but first open your present."

Paul cringed each time I ripped a piece of *Superman #1*. I pulled a hardcover edition of the brand-new comic book price guide out of the wrapping.

"I know you like comics, so I bought you that," Dad said. "You can thank Mom for the wrapping. I asked her to find some wrapping paper that you might like, and sure enough, she left me this reproduction of an old *Superman* comic. I don't know where your mom gets stuff, but she can find just about anything."

Confused, Mom looked over to the pile of colorful paper decorated with pacifier-chewing baby ducks that still lay on Dad's desk.

Mom and Dad went upstairs to fix breakfast. Paul ran to the bathroom and made a horrible retching noise. I turned to the back of the price guide and saw an article on how much all the old comic books were worth. A caption read, "The first comic starring Batman recently sold at auction for $165,000. It was sold by Mr. Somerset, of Springs, Long Island." A picture showed Mr. Somerset holding a bunch of old comic books in one hand. In his other hand he held the comic book price guide with a smiley face on the cover, the one Paul had dropped back in 1939!

I wasn't upset at all.

For the four days since we got back from the future, I had thought that my dad's most valuable possession was rescued, and that he didn't hate me anymore. Now it turned out that things weren't really any different—Dad's favorite possession was still wrecked, and it was still my fault. But for four days I didn't feel guilty about it, and things were perfect.

When Paul came back in from the bathroom, I announced, "Things are back to normal!"

He moaned, "I know, *Superman #1* is wrecked."

Over breakfast, Dad made all sorts of corny jokes and fooled around like always. It was so obvious that he wasn't faking his feelings toward me that I felt silly for all the years of worrying. He made a face on his plate using bacon for a mouth, eggs for the eyes, and sausage for the nose. Then he made it say, "Happy birthday, Brian!" in a high-pitched voice. Paul and I laughed so hard that milk came out of our noses.

The next day I went to visit Mr. Somerset. He pulled up his sleeve to show me a big tattoo of a Lamborghini with the license plate "SMRSET." He said he was going to retire soon, after he sold the rest of his rare, golden-age comics.

That night I read the TimeQuest comic. Every page was filled in, down to the very last panel. The last few pages showed our adventures in the far future and, of course, my discovery that Dad didn't secretly hate me. The artist even drew a light bulb over my head! The very last panel showed the world crumbling behind Nathan as he begged us to change things. The caption read, "Will our heroes save the world?"

The TimeQuest ring disappeared from my finger, and the TimeQuest coins vanished into thin air. The title on the cover changed from *TimeQuest* to *The Comic Book Kid: A One-Issue Adventure*. Even though it was a little beat up, I put the comic in a protective bag. After all, there's only one of them, and it could be worth something someday. I'm going to put it in a bank vault after I grow up and have my own kids.

Now there's just one last problem. Mr. O asked us to write a story for homework using all that we learned in class about characters, dialogue, setting, conflicts, and a bunch of other things. Well, I missed a lot of what he said about that stuff because I was too busy writing notes to Paul and feeding chocolate to a mutant in my backpack, but I can't wait to see the look on his face when I hand him this big book.

The End